THE BOOK OF MAYA

A VAMPIRE HUNTERS ACADEMY NOVEL

DELIZHIA JENKINS

The Book of Maya

Copyright © 2022 by Delizhia Jenkins

All rights reserved.

No part of this book may be reproduced in any form or by any electronic or mechanical means, including information storage and retrieval systems, without written permission from the author, except for the use of brief quotations in a book review.

Cover Designed by Nicole Shepherd

ACKNOWLEDGMENTS

In 2003, I never would have imagined that I would be the proud author of one book, let alone nineteen. To the eighteen year old young woman, who knew very little about the world outside of your household, who looked to the future with a heart full of hope and a million dreams that was kept tucked away in your pocket, you did it. You did what your soul called out for you to do. You were bold. You were brave. You were determined. You learned to fight even when you were afraid to clench a fist. Into the darkness you dove, without even the small flickering of light from a candle, you found your way to the woman you were destined to become. When you were overlooked by those who claimed to love you, you continued on with your journey. When no one even attempted to understand you, you eventually learned to understand yourself. You didn't break. You didn't give up. And I am so proud of you.

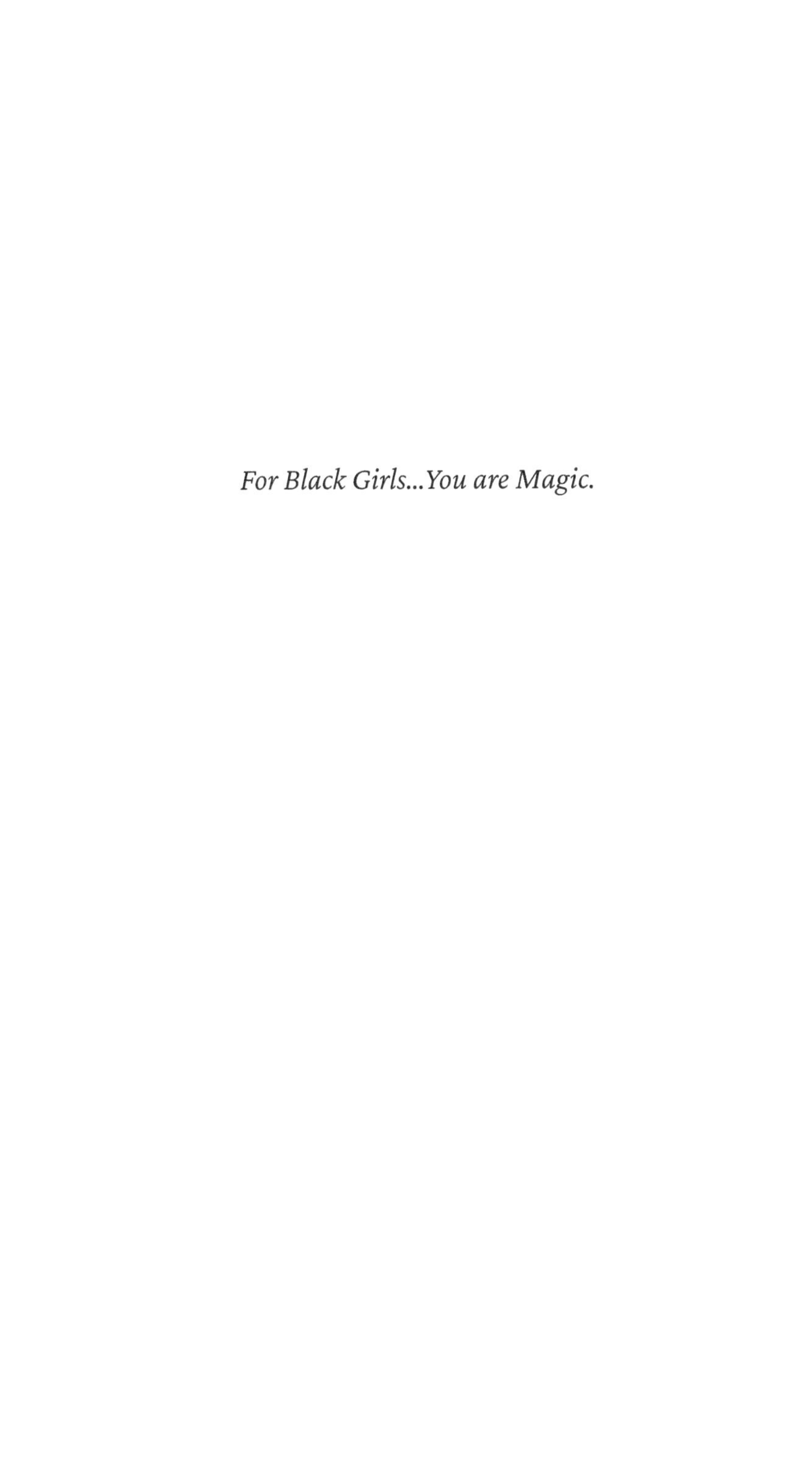

For Black Girls...You are Magic.

PROLOGUE

November 2, 2015

Present Day

Sometimes, I pretend that my life began when I arrived at The Vampire Hunters Academy. If I were to organize the events that took place before The Academy, I label those moments as B.A- Before the Academy. And the events that took place after my arrival, well that is when everything I once knew, disappeared into the shadows of the past-my A.A. (After the Academy) moments. I used to pretend that I could live in a world without magic, a world without vampires and demons, and witches, and rituals... Staring out of the window, watching the other girls play Double-Dutch outside of my house, totally oblivious to the fact that my mother sacrificed a goat just moments before they spun the rope. They skipped, while I cried silently as the house rumbled in response to a demon answering my mother's call. They sang silly songs, and I was forced to learn incantations to assist with binding spells and curses.

And then I watched them disappear into each other's homes for tea parties, sleepovers and trips that their parents eagerly took them on. Meanwhile, my mother used me to assist with collecting payment from the married patrons that would often visit our two story plantation styled home, that sought at least one of my mother's many services.

My childhood was a far cry from childlike. I did things, saw things, and heard things that no child should ever witness. I was told that I was destined to be the most powerful witch of our bloodline. As a matter of fact, despite many of the depravities, every witch in our coven treated me as if I were royalty. However, some of them knew a secret I didn't. As a matter of fact, some of my coven sisters in that hell hole knew more about my destiny than me – and I was the one destined to live it.

The days that followed the Guardians rescuing me and brought me to The Vampire Hunters Academy was both the best and worst days of my life. I was free of my mother's abuse, her plots, and her schemes. But still, I wasn't free of the power that burned its way through my veins or the burden that came with it. The day my mother was dragged out of the cemetery, her ankles bound by iron shackles, her hands cuffed and covered with blessed cloths; her head low and the slow whisper of curses being muttered under her breath was the day I realized it wasn't over. She wasn't done with me.

And even as I sit in my first period class waiting for my best friend to hurry up and sit with me, I can still hear my mother's voice in the backdrop of my mind reminding me that I still have a duty to fulfill; and regardless of how many miles I put between myself and my past, I will never be truly free. The hour will come for when it is time for the gates of Hell to be opened and the plague of a prophecy that looms over my bloodline will be fulfilled. However, I am a proud New Orleans witch nonetheless and the day that I have to confront Samael, I will be more than happy to demonstrate exactly what this New Orleans *witch* can do.

Eleven Years Ago...

French toast. I love how it smells more than I love the taste. The pure sweetness of it is an aroma that I simply cannot get enough of. It's the only reminder of normalcy I have before my day begins with harvesting the eyes of a salamander for a spell or spending the morning being taught how to properly conjure up a demon for bidding purposes. Or worse, how to look another grown man in the eye when he winks as he passes me, following behind one of my coven sisters into one of the many rooms of the plantation home that has been in our family since the eighteen hundred's.

Not only is my coven composed of thirteen witches of varying degrees of strengths and abilities; my coven also provides brothel services... I have seen certain celebrities, politicians even, and wealthy men and women from all over the world come through our doors seeking help with love potions, hexes, cleansings, protection...but those same celebrities have also spent nights here under the comfort of the adult women who served under the leadership of my mother, Marguerite Beauvais. High Priestess of the House of Beauvais, Grand Witch and powerful servant of the dark and the hidden. My mother is also gifted in many other practices and possesses a lot of knowledge on Druid magic.

But see, my mother has also taken what is called a Dark Oath, which grants her an awfully large amount of power and access into the lower realms. Demons themselves fear her just like many of the other covens that operate here in Louisiana. I've been told that I am supposed to "follow in her footsteps" of dark greatness, but to be honest, I'm not sure if I want to... the magic she performs... scares me. There have been nights when I couldn't sleep because the spirits of the recently deceased would speak to me. Many of them victims of my mother.

As a matter of fact, when in the presence of "company" I am to refer to her as the other members of our esteemed coven: High Priestess. Very rarely was I allowed to call her "mom". From birth I was passed down to be raised by one of her handmaids, who were more like apprentices than anything else. Camille had proven to be more of a mother than I could have imagined; she put kindness above her craft which would often infuriate the High Priestess. Camille's clients would even tip her more than the other girls and it was not uncommon for her to be on the receiving end of an extravagant gift such as a BMW. I remember hearing about one of her clients who actually *fell in love* with her and offered to marry her.

However, I am not sure if it was really her loyalty to our coven or her fear of my mother that made her tearfully decline his offer. But I remember being in her arms as she wept over the phone. I remember wrapping my arms around her hoping that would be enough to help soothe her pain. Five year old me could not understand the depth of her sacrifice, but even then, I knew it wasn't fair.

Life for any witch – at least in our coven – wasn't fair.

But back to French toast...

"Maya, I am going to need you to assist Hacienda with tonight's moon ritual," my mother announced as she entered the kitchen. "And since you will be out, head on over to the closest bayou, and collect several jars of dirt. The faster you get there, the faster I will be able to prepare for tonight..."

Camille had just finished making me breakfast: French toast, eggs, a bowl of fruit and a cup of orange juice when my mother, The High Priestess appeared in the doorway. She always commanded attention even without uttering a word. I looked up at her, my mouth full of French toast and eggs, slightly surprised that she even knew I was alive.

"What kind of ritual are we doing tonight mom?" I asked curiously as I slid off the high, wooden chair and quickly approached her.

She regarded me with a tickle of amusement and for a moment, I thought that maybe, she could step out of "Priestess mode" and just be...my mom.

"We are doing a combination of things really... mostly reinforcing our protection barriers, but with the thinning of the veil, it is important that we pay an old ancestor a tribute tonight." She paused and rested her shoulder against the fridge. "But don't worry about that right now. Just finish your breakfast. Hacienda is in the Garden finishing up the recipe for a spell."

That got my attention. Hacienda's magic was amazing, and I loved to watch her perform her spell work. I turned toward the table, my feet slapping against the marble floor and reached for toast and took another huge bite before guzzling down my orange juice. Hacienda was also the youngest working witch in our coven – eighteen. She came to us when she was fifteen and a runaway from her abusive stepfather.

"Ok," I managed to gulp.

"Make sure you both are back before sunset. Evil comes alive when the sun sets," my mother warned before turning away, her robe billowing behind her.

"Ok," I repeated, unsure if she even heard me or not. I continued to stuff my face with what remained of my French toast and eggs, before abandoning the table all together. I already expect a scolding later on today either from Camille or one of my other "sisters" for leaving my plate on the table. But I'm anxious to spend time with Hacienda. I want her to teach me how to work with the elements – fire to be exact.

I quickly dart off and up the stairs to my room to change out of my nightgown when I bypass the cracked door of my mother's room. Usually, she is pretty guarded about who enters her room, going as far as to locking it shut with a spell. But the opportunity and just good old fashioned curiosity encouraged me to tip closer to her room and stand next to her door. My heart raced as I gently pressed the side of my face against the door. At first, the voices were muffled but judging from the distorted tone, my mother had conjured up a demon. I hate working with demons. They are scary and loud…and sometimes, its dangerous for a weaker witch to summon one on her own. We lost one of our sisters once because she refused to ask for help while summoning. The demon managed to break the pentagram she drew to contain him and as a result he took possession of her body. It took the strength of my mother and two other experienced witches to release her; but not before he snapped her neck.

"…she is not ready yet," I heard my mother say evenly. "The agreement was when she comes into full power on her twenty first birthday…"

Who is she talking about? I think to myself.

"I can feel her power even from beyond the Gates," the garbled voice challenged. "Her blood is strong."

"Her blood is only potent enough to break the seal," my mother argued. "I am a woman of my word-"

"You and your pathetic bloodline owe me a great deal of debt," the voice continued. "I gave you the power that you possess. I have waited centuries for my freedom."

"And you will have that," my mother promised. "You will be free-"

"There is only so much time and patience I have left to afford Marguerite," the entity growled. "Your mother had promised me that you would be the key; but your blood is *weak...*"

I could feel my mother cringe at his remark, and I wondered what level of demon she was working with.

"She has to learn her magic to prepare the way," my mother stammered. "She will not be able to open the gates if she cannot yield her own power."

"She has until her sixteenth birthday Marguerite," the demon asserted. "If the earth does not taste the blood of Maya Beauvais-"

I cup my mouth as I silently release a gasp. *I'm*

the sacrifice? Why?

"...even from the darkest pits I will wage war against you, old witch. Your enemies will become my consorts; I will strip you of your magic and leave you destitute in the street like the whore that you are. I will send the most twisted of demons to feed on your spirit while the blood drinkers and Rougarou feast on your flesh."

"Yes, Samael," my mother said softly. "As you wish."

It was in that moment that I understood why my mother treated me as nothing more than an obligation. I was born to act as a sacrifice to an entity that my mother, Marguerite Giselle Beauvais, High Priestess and Queen of the French Quarter served. A living goddess who bowed before a greater god... the irony.

And even then, at my age-five, I knew I had to escape. One way or another, I had to get out of that brothel and far away from my mother. In that moment, as I silently tip-toed away from her door to go back to my room, I realized that my mother was no longer my mother, but Marguerite. And from that day forward, I learned the importance of time – something, that I could easily and very quickly exhaust if I didn't come up with something.

"Hurry up Maya," Hacienda urged as she slid out of the Honda Civic, yanking her satchel filled with several empty glass jars for us to collect the dirt in. My excitement for this journey was still haunted by what was at stake: my life. My mother was really going to sacrifice me to a demon on my sixteenth birthday. I struggled to fight back tears and I wished that Camille was with me instead of Hacienda. As much as I loved to witness Hacienda work with her magic, her magic would not be enough to save me.

Especially when it came to the High Priestess.

Reluctantly I slid out of the car and followed behind Hacienda who marched into the marshy area. As soon as my feet touched the wet ground, my palms instantly become sweaty and clammy. Voices from the earth surrounded me, the trapped souls of the deceased, called out to me, pleading with me to set them free...to avenge them...to bring comfort to their pain. Clutching my head, I tried to blot out the loud, incessant mourning, but the pain held me in its grip. In my head, I could see the translucent, ghastly forms of the dead; I can smell the blood that oozed from the dirt, resurfacing like a nightmare in the belly of the subconscious. So much death... horrendous murders took place here on the bayou that every stretch of this land has become an unmarked grave.

"Maya!" Hacienda called out to me. I closed my eyes and tried to ground myself as Camille had taught me, but this was too much. And then the form of a small child, probably no older than me reached out. Her tiny arms begged me to hold her.

I screamed.

Hacienda scooped me into her arms and held me. *"Spiritus esse abiit!"* she called out, waving her hand. *"Nulla contentio, cum te."*

Almost instantly the spirits disappeared along with the wailing. "Are you alright?" Hacienda asked, examining my face and wiping away the tears.

"I don't know," I tell her. "I could feel them…they were sad."

"I know. It sucks. One day you and me will have to come back and do a releasing spell. Many of the native souls and souls of the African slaves are trapped here." She paused and continued to look at me. "Hey you're pretty strong, kid."

I stopped sniffling and glance up at Hacienda curiously. "I am?"

"Yeah, you're not even six years old and already you can commune with the dead. Necromancy is definitely one of your gifts. Your mother is going to be really proud of you."

Just the mere mention of my mother made me cringe. "Please don't tell her about my new powers," I hear myself whisper.

Hacienda sat me down on the hood of her car and studied me. "She would be proud of you though," she said, offering a smile. "Like I'm proud of you. Your mother is a bad ass, kid."

I begin to shake my head. "I don't think so. She doesn't love me like Camille does."

"She is just busy, that's all. It's a lot of work to run a coven as large and as powerful as ours. You are going to follow in her footsteps one day, kid. You will see. Come on, lets go grab some dirt before it gets dark."

She reaches into her bag and hands me a jar, which I reluctantly accept and follow behind her. Even with her spell, I could still feel the presence of the souls, their voices a soft whisper compared to the mournful wails that echoed in my ear drums. A sense of dread crawled its way up my spine and sent tremors down to my fingertips. I was torn between wanting to abandon my jars and go home or stay here with the spirits.

Hacienda picked a random spot that was just a few feet away from the river. "Watch out for alligators," she said stooping down. "And hurry up! This place gives me the heebee jeebies."

CHAPTER

THREE

I never wanted to be a witch. What I wanted was to be able to play hopscotch with the other girls down the street and eat ice cream outside after we played in the sprinklers all day. I wanted to go to the neighborhood school and be with other kids and laugh and joke and play tag and dance...I wanted to wear pretty, lacy dresses and attend Sunday sermon like the other kids in the neighborhood. But Sunday sermons conflicted with the practices of our coven, and of my bloodline.

My mother even bragged about hexing a preacher once.

I remember the day he violently knocked on our door. The rich scent of his expensive cologne filtered into our foyer. I was standing next to the old piano that needed more than just tune-up, while Morgana was busy with a tarot reading for one of her clients. She popped her head up to glance at the door. All the clairvoyants had sensed him right before he raised his fist to pound on the wooden frame of the door. We kept our curtains closed most of the time just as a precaution against our sometimes nosey neighbors, but I could still "see" him and his two accomplices. Anxiety forced me away from the piano and I began to retreat as my mother's footsteps could be heard coming up the stairs.

He knocked again, only pausing to look at his gold Rolex. The two female supporters of his gripped their bibles tightly to their chests. I looked over at Morgana who shrugged.

"Don't' worry," my mother said evenly just as her foot reached the last step. She calmly removed her head wrap to expose her waist long curly hair. Her loosely fitted white dress still did not hide her soft curves, or the roundness of her hips and the fullness of her bosom. Both men and women found my mother irresistible, and it would be no surprise that the pastor would not have a natural defense against her magnetic beauty.

When it came to dealing with the opposite sex, my mother moved with the patience of a King

Cobra. She would lie and wait for her target to get close enough for her to strike, and when she did, it was fast, hard, and venomous. And a man of the cloth would be no exception to her dangerous game. Morgana and I could only watch as she gently opened the door just as he continued to hit it with a hard bang. She opened the door wide enough for both the pastor and his minions to have a full view of the interior of our home.

"Good afternoon," she smiled. "How may I help you?"

For a moment, the pastor appeared transfixed as he carefully regarded her from head to toe. One of his minions cleared her throat and offered him a slight nudge to remind him of his purpose.

"Goo-good afternoon," he stammered. "May I speak with the head of the household?"

"You are speaking to her," my mother said. "My name is Marguerite Beauvais, Head Mistress and High Priestess of the House of Beauvais. Are you interested in any of our services?"

"We are not here for your *services* Ms. Beauvais," the pastor said quickly. "I am Pastor Findley from St. Luke Baptist Church just a few blocks away from here."

"And what exactly brings you to my doorstep?" My mother asked, folding her arms across her chest.

"We are well aware of this house of *sin* Ms. Beauvais," one of his minions spat, waving her King James bible in my mother's face.

"Well, if you are aware of my business dealings here, I would be careful about where you point that bible, Mrs. Johnson," my mother said coolly. The tension thickened between the three of them, and I could see my mother's hair begin to crackle with energy.

"We have come here to offer you an opportunity towards salvation," Pastor Findley declared, holding his head up.

Morgana and I shared an uneasy glance. I could only imagine my mother's facial expression as she regarded his offer.

"Salvation," my mother repeated, slightly titling her head. Her demeanor remained indifferent which probably increased the pastor's already mounting anxiety.

"Yes," Pastor Findley continued. "One of my parishioners was a recent..." he paused to clear his throat. "Guest in your home."

"Is that right?"

"His *wife* came to us and told us that you put a curse on him," Mrs. Johnson spat.

"Thou shall not suffer a witch to live," said the other flunky. "Exodus 33:8-10…"

"A curse?" My mother said softly, her gaze switching from Pastor Findley to the older woman known as Mrs. Johnson.

My heart began to race when my mother fell silent. Telepathically, I could hear her murmuring words of a spell.

"And she has a child in the house!" Mrs. Johnson pressed, adjusting her sound frame to where her eyes could meet mine. "This is a house of *hell-* no place for a child."

"So, you are here, standing on my property to condemn me with your own self- righteousness regarding business that does not concern you or your ministry?" My mother's voice began to gain strength as she held her gaze on Mrs. Johnson. "And to further add insult to injury, you have laid your eyes onto a child that did not come from your womb – as your womb is about as barren as a dead field – and my child to be exact-"

"I will not tolerate the soothe sayings of a witch!" Mrs. Johnson gasped.

"And you claim to come here with an offering of

salvation based on the ramblings of a jealous, insecure and possibly insufferable wife? *Who* is going to offer me, this salvation exactly?" My mother asked, taking a step outside.

"Our Heavenly Father," Pastor Findley stammered, taking a step back. He motioned for the two women to do the same. "We did not come here to cause trouble."

"But you did," my mother continued. "You come here to offer me salvation on behalf of another deity that I know nothing about. Your lord is your lord." She paused and through my mind's eye I could sense the devious smile spreading across her face. "Tell me your sins, Pastor?"

I felt the power of my mother's kinetic energy wrap around Pastor Findley like an invisible cord, holding him in place.

"Let him go!" Mrs. Johnson challenged. "Holy Father, I ask that you banish this demon..."

As soon as she uttered those words, my mother shouted, "*Adolebit!* (burn)" and the very King James bible that she held tightly in her grip went up in flames. Mrs. Johnson screamed and released the book and watched in horror as the fire consumed it. My mother released a hard laugh and used the same force to bind the two accomplices next to Pastor Findley.

"Now," my mother continued. "Tell me your sins…"

Pastor Findley struggled against the pull of her magic, but quickly realized that it was to no avail.

"I bore two children outside of my marriage that my wife knows nothing about," he reluctantly confessed. "By a woman who is also married…"

He fought back tears as he glanced at the stunned expressions of his two supporters. "She is married to my best friend of fifteen years…"

"Tell me more Pastor Findley," my mother cooed. "Tell me your deepest, darkest secrets…"

Pastor Findley began to sob uncontrollably as his mouth muscles struggled to not reveal the dark truth that remained trapped in his throat. "Please," he managed to say. "Please…"

"Don't be shy," my mother taunted. "The truth will set you free…"

"I-I-I deceive the younger women in the church who seek me out for counsel," he stammered. "In exchange for my counsel, they have to pay, because I am a man of God."

"And how do you have them pay?" My mother pressed.

"I tell them that in order to get to God, they have to go through me. And the only way they can get to God through me is through sex."

"So, you make these women prostitute themselves for God," my mother inquired. She doubled over in laughter, gripping her sides, she struggled to silence her merriment. I was willing to bet that her voice echoed all the way into the very bayous of Louisiana.

"That's what you are telling me," she managed to say after her bout of amusement began to die down.

He continues to sob and doesn't say anything. My mother then turns to Mrs. Johnson and says, "Tell me your sins..."

"I lied about my sister's husband," she said mournfully. "I wanted him. I wanted him badly. But he chose her, just like everyone else does... Ten years ago, I told my father that he had raped me. I showed him my bloodied underwear that I had from my menstrual as evidence...my father tracked him down and shot him twice...and now my father is serving a life sentence..."

"You wicked, WICKED woman!" my mother squealed, clapping her hands. She turned around to look at Morgana and said, "And they call *me* a witch." My mother spun around to face the other woman. But this time, she didn't command the woman to reveal her dark truths. I could hear my mother searching through the woman's mind. Whatever it was she uncovered, made her release the woman.

"You are the only one who stands before me, innocent of your convictions," my mother said evenly. "I can't even be mad at you for being a sheep. But if I were you, I'd find another church. And leave people like me alone." My mother paused before shooing her away. "Go. And do not let me find you on this street ever again. To do so, will be at your own risk."

The woman looked at Pastor Findley and Mrs. Johnson, both of which were pleading with their eyes for her to leave. Without a word the woman dumped her bible in the grass and sprung off our porch, her high heeled feet hit the ground so hard, she could be heard racing down the street.

"Now for the two of you," My mother said as she paced back and forth. "What will I do with you?"

"Please... please let us go..." Pastor Findley begged.

"Oh you will be released safe and sound... but not before I say this: *Maledictum enim est, maledictum pro duo* (A curse for one is a curse for two) *sit omne mendacium locutus veri* (let every lie spoken become true) *Et ut corda eorum in te amorem esse repletus ira* (may the hearts of those you love be filled with rage) *et sit bonum non invenire te* (and let no good find you) *et sit spiritibus defunctorum colunt vos pro reliquis diebus vestris* (and let the spirits of the dead haunt you for the rest of your days)... *Non est salus, pro iacentem homo vel mulier zelus* (There is no salvation for a lying man or a jealous woman)."

She stopped to face Mrs. Johnson who trembled before her. "Your womb is dead, just like you will be soon. That will be the perfect time to apologize to your brother-in-law. His spirit speaks to me now and he is disgusted with you."

Her gaze returned to Pastor Findley who had soiled his pants. My mother frowned. "You also disgust me. I may not be a gatekeeper to heaven, but I surely am the doorman to hell. *Infernum est, quod te vivere et inferno, ubi est vobis vado* (Hell is what you live, and hell is where you shall go.)."

My mother turned around and with a wave of her hand, she released them. She said nothing more as she closed the door behind her. But not long after that day, St. Luke Baptist church closed its doors for good due to a fire that broke out. It was said that

Pastor Findley lost everything; his wife found out about his affairs and divorced him. And the husband of the woman with whom he had the long standing affair and the children by, approached him inside a bar one evening and shot him twice in the back of the head.

And as for Mrs. Johnson...

Her name was a topic for conversation within my coven many nights after her encounter with my mother. My mother cursed her with an invisible marker which is the equivalent to a bull's eye target within her aura. She became a beacon for darkness, and it would be a matter of time before she was driven to madness by an Incubi or Succubi; or perhaps she would be taken as a gift to the devil himself by the Loogaroo; or she would find herself kissed by a demon and afflicted with disease that would cause both her body and soul to rot...but none of those things came to be. Instead, she caught the attention of a vampire, one that enjoyed cat and mouse games with his victims. It is said for three days, he toyed with her. He made appearances in her dreams, watched her from the shadows of the trees that surrounded her townhome. She went as far as to try to seek help from law enforcement, but without a clear ID of her "stalker" or any supporting information that justified her terror, there was nothing they could do. And on the fourth hour of the early morning on the fourth day, he lured her outside, using his voice like that of a siren to an unsuspecting sailor.

And he drained her of every drop of blood she possessed before he snapped her neck…right in the middle of her own backyard.

Mrs. Johnson and Pastor Findley were just two examples of what happens when Marguerite Giselle Beauvais is crossed. Word continued to spread about my mother's power, and it would not be long before our coven found itself front row center of a resurrected feud between my mother and an old enemy of hers. But even as our House prepared for every kind of psychic attack imaginable, an all out affront would never reach our doorstep. And it would only be a matter of time before the rest of my coven would understand why.

FOUR

Hacienda's loud, off key voice hovered over the sound of Britney Spears, "Toxic" as we made our way home from the bayou. The sun was beginning its slow retreat beneath the horizon, which was motivation enough for her to keep her foot pressed on the accelerator. Plus, the silent threat of punishment from my mother if we were late to tonight's ceremony was enough of a motivator in and of itself. Each member of our coven has suffered the harsh hand of my mother's punishment at one point or another, except for me. I cringed at the invading thought as we made a quick turn towards the exit ramp.

My mother led our coven with an iron fist – this was fact. Most of the women fell under her leadership when they came running and screaming from the demons that haunted them. Some of those demons being predatory stepfathers and abusive mothers, former pimps and drug dealers, and other coven leaders. Each of my coven sisters have placed my mother's protection above everything, including their own freedom. Morgana for instance, came to us, desperate to escape not just the iron clad grasp of her pimp, Nigel- whose reputation was human trafficking, and the sale of black market drugs- but his life as a creature was of the night- a vampire.

It was said that Morgana was his most prized property; her youth and vibrant Celtic beauty is what drew in huge amounts of profit from powerful men of all walks of life. He also used Morgana's ability to read minds, which is how this vampire was able to avoid the blessed blades of Guardians or find himself a pile of ash by the hands of his enemies. Morgana was only sixteen at the time she gathered enough courage to make her escape into the daylight. She used her gift as a means to slip past his guards and make her way onto the streets. She managed to escape New York under the cover of day and into New Jersey where she sought refuge with another coven for a few short weeks before Nigel found her.

I remember hearing my sisters whisper the retelling of her story, when Nigel, a centuries old vampire who even had his hand in the African slave trade, slaughtered all thirteen members of that coven. She barely succeeded in her escape, once again at daybreak, running and hiding until after two months of going from place to place and never staying more than a single night, she put out a mental telepathic call for help. Other covens had heard about Nigel's reign of terror but refused to involve themselves with a vampire as old as him. They regarded it as a "Guardian" problem, something that other covens also preferred to avoid by any means necessary. A witch on the run from a vampire was not an uncommon theme in our world, and Morgana would not be an exception.

The night that Nigel found Morgana, she was hiding in an abandoned motel in North Carolina. Unbeknownst to either of them, Marguerite had received the SOS from the baby witch and decided to investigate. As the story goes, my mother left Camille in charge of business, while she went out to examine the threat that prompted Morgana to call out for help. And sure enough, Marguerite, grand-witch of the House of Beauvais, chosen Bride of Darkness, appeared just in time to stop Nigel in his tracks from laying another hand on Morgana. It is said that Morgana was beaten to near unconsciousness when Marguerite stripped Nigel of his own flesh before setting his remains on fire with the flick of her hand.

Morgana came to our coven just a few years before I was born, but from what I heard, Marguerite had to transport her back to our home, where she was tended to by Camille, Janelle and Beatrice – all who had served under my mother for years. It wasn't until Morgana had fully recovered when she pledged her full allegiance to the House of Beauvais. Now, Morgana services men of her choosing, but prefers to profit from her "gift". Under my mother's tutelage, Morgana has learned how to access other powers using tarot and other mediums of varying crafts.

But even with Morgana's welcoming into our coven as a new initiate, she too would learn the price that came with my mother's protection – just as Hacienda would be reminded of such tonight. I sat back and tried not to think about the setting of the sun, which was another rule. We could not be out after sunset on any given day, unless instructed to do so. It's true that vampires infest the bayous, small towns and cities of Louisiana. Only a strong witch is an even match against an older vampire, but still, the life of a witch should have offered unadulterated freedom. Instead, however, the life of a witch was often quite the contrary. If we aren't killed by our stronger and powerful peers, vampires, demons, and even an incorrectly performed spell, a witch's life was all too often cut short. This is the secret that is often whispered within the private confines of a spelled room amongst one's closest allies. And while most covens offered the stable protection of an invisible cage, the House of Beauvais was a beautiful prison.

"Shit," Hacienda cursed as she glanced at her sideview mirror. "I knew we should have taken a different route. We are going to be late."

Cold terror shot through my veins as I shifted in my seat. "Can't you just drive faster Hacienda?" I asked.

"It's not that simple kid," she said evenly. "For whatever reason traffic is gridlocked."

"But the full moon is tonight!"

"I know! The moon isn't due to rise until 11:00, so we have time...it's just..."

"Vampires?" I asked.

"Not just that...Guardians. We are close to one of their compounds. I can feel it. They will be out tonight, in droves."

"Why are Guardians so bad? Vampires kill people. Guardians kill vampires."

"They just don't kill vampires' kid," Hacienda tells me as she maneuvered her way around an SUV and into the next lane which placed her closer to the light. "They capture witches like us and try to force us to convert to their religion and sometimes, they kill us too."

That shut me up. I had heard a few stories about Guardians interrupting the livelihoods of covens in the name of the Vatican. My mother referred to them as "New Age Crusaders" and even though they did what they could to keep the vampire populations at bay, they were still a viable threat- at least to her.

Hacienda's Honda was finally allowed to move forward another few feet before once again coming to a stop. "Fuck! Come on, move!"

After another seemingly long wait, traffic relaxed, and Hacienda was able to push forward, and we were able to release hard sighs of relief. Twenty minutes later, we pulled in front our home, just in time before the last ray of light sank beneath the horizon. I hopped out the car with two of the dirt filled jars in my arms, careful not to drop them as I made my approach to the front porch. Marguerite emerged from the front door and our eyes locked. Her calm gaze paralyzed me in the middle of our front lawn; frozen like a statue with the two jars held firmly in my grip.

Does she know that I know? I think to myself. *Oh no! She probably can hear my thoughts!* I panicked. *She knows!*

"Maya," my mother said gently. "Why are you just standing there? Bring the jars inside. I need to begin my work now."

My sweaty palms made it difficult to hold onto to the jars, however there would be no way I would allow myself to drop them. I forced myself to move and each step felt more awkward as I approached the porch.

"Are you alright Maya?" My mother asked, surveying me.

"She is probably still a little spooked," Hacienda offered as she came up behind me.

"What happened?"

"Well, as soon we hopped out of the car in the bayou, she tapped in with the spirits of the dead," Hacienda continued proudly. "She's definitely going to be a powerful witch someday."

My mother offered a knowing smile. "She is...she is a Beauvais. I would expect nothing less."

FIVE

I spent the remainder of the evening hiding out in my room while my mother and the rest of our coven harnessed the energy of the full moon to reinforce the protection barriers that were placed around our property. I buried myself underneath my covers, closed my eyes as I imagined running into the waiting arms of my faceless father. During nights like these, when our house rattled and whistled and shifted from the effects of the magic that coated every wooden panel, floorboard, window, doorway, room, all the way down to the very fiber of the carpets, I would visualize my life as a mundane human girl. No gifts. No magic. No demons. No vampires. In my mind, a handsomely built and well- dressed man with soft curly hair, café au lait skin, and a velvety baritone voice would scoop me up with kisses and hugs in the foyer. He would greet me with a small bouquet of flowers he purchased on his way home and in those moments, I would feel safe. He would then leave his brief case in the doorway and the woman I imagined to be my mother, would emerge out of the kitchen, her apron dirty from spending the last two hours preparing dinner and the two would greet each other with a simple kiss and a smile.

My perfect family...

And speaking of my father, a man with honey brown skin and a warm smile used to pay our home a visit almost weekly. My memories of him are vague, reduced to nothing more than an apparition of a feeling, a presence, a whisper of a thought. But I remember the rich scent of his cologne mixed with the smoke of his cigar. He was one of the few patrons my mother personally tended to and her main client. He would always arrive at the time I was seated at the table, eating dinner. And he would gaze at me appreciatively, ask me about my day and proceed to leave a single pink rose next to my plate. His eyes were similar in shape, as was his mouth and smile...they were like mine. He stood proudly with a set of broad shoulders and height to match.

One evening as I had come down later than usual for dinner that Camille had prepared for me, I overheard him speaking with my mother at the bottom of the stairway. I crept lightly so as not to interrupt their conversation and I pressed my small body against the wall.

"...she should come live with me and my family," he expressed sternly to my mother. "This is no place for a girl child to be raised."

"And you are in no place to come to such conclusions," my mother countered evenly. "Besides, what would your *wife* think?"

"She is well aware of my wrong doings," he said without hesitation. "But she loves me anyway. I told her about Maya, and she is open to extending our home to her. Maya will be cared for in every way imaginable. She will have a good life, she will become educated, and I will see to it that she marries well."

"Marries well? To whom? What good is a marriage when married men find their way into my bed?"

"I refuse to stand by and allow this child to become a lady of the night," the man said quickly, his tone sharpening.

"Oh, but the night is so beautiful," my mother

taunted. And just like a viper, she recoiled, and I could almost imagine her fangs visible and prepared to strike. "I have given you everything that a man of your ilk could imagine; comfort when you wife is unable to perform her wifely duties; power, money to support your family – including the beautiful Dahlia who wears her wedding ring ever so proudly...why, now that I think of it, she is more my wife than yours. I can taste her sweet nectar every single time you –

"That is enough Marguerite!" He snapped; his eyes lit with fury. I peered around the corner to see the two of them locked in a heated stare down. He surprised me with his lack of fear towards my mother. Most men would have cowered by now. "You and I both know that you do not want or need a child –

"I love my daughter very much," my mother quipped. "Here she is safe, here she is secure; here she will become powerful in her own right -without the burden of being a man's wife. In time, she will be able to weave worlds that are bound to her command...not have to bow to the position of a man."

"You do not love that child Marguerite," he hissed. "You have no idea what love is."

"And you do?"

"I know a hell of a lot more than you do when it comes to the well being of a child," he pressed. "She is nothing more than a tool for whatever wicked game you have up your sleeve."

"And what game is that? See, here is what I reckon, *mon cher*," my mother began. "You, Daniel O. H. Morgan, the rising political star, no longer the lowly insurance broker, who could barely afford the upkeep of his mortgage is now worried that word would soon spread about his extracurricular activities in a rumored house of magic."

"At this point, I don't give a damn Marguerite. She deserves a better life than this."

"A life better than what exactly? Hmm? A life better than the hand that I gave you? I think it is time for you to leave Daniel."

There was a pause. "You are not the only witch in this town," he growled.

"How much are you really willing to sacrifice just to think you can win a war with me Mr. Morgan? What price are you willing to pay to another witch with half the power I have at my disposal?"

"One way or another Marguerite, I will come for

her," Daniel promised. I continued to peek around the corner to watch him reach for his briefcase.

"I commend you for even wanting to fulfill your blooded role as her father. But you are done here. Go. Be happy Daniel. Maya is not your business…"

I stood transfixed as my mother's eyes turned abysmal black and Daniel's horrified expression suddenly became serene. She paralyzed him with her gaze; he began to sway slightly as if his will struggled to fight for control over his mind.

"Hinc et numquam redire (leave here and never return)," my mother whispered. "Oblivisci eius (forget about her). Illa non est filia tua, amplius (she is not your daughter anymore). Vade in domum tuam uxorem et non loqui in nomine meo iterum (go home to your wife and do not speak my name ever again…"

And just like that she released him. My heart hurt, silently begging him to stay and fight. How dare she send my father away! Why would she do that? Why did she hate me so much that she would deny me the one chance to experience love at least from one of my parents? I watched him snap out of her gaze, smile, remove his hat with a bow and reach for his briefcase.

"It's been a pleasure mistress," he said cheerfully, as if he had not just engaged in a heated conversation with the most powerful witch in Louisiana. This would be the last time I would see his face and connect with eyes that matched mine. "Until next time..."

My mother returned the smile. "Until next time..."

The day that I learned the identity of my father was the day I watched him walk away. The only reminder I have of him is the pink rose that he would leave at the table for me. That's another favorite thing of mine: pink roses. French toast and pink roses. Every time I come across a pink rose, I think of Daniel, and I wonder if the little girl with the thick mane of curls he came to visit every week at the plantation home crosses his mind too, even if he cannot remember why.

There was a time when the nightmares were nothing but haunted moments of sleep that would eventually seep away when the light came. I could always hear things that went bump in the night. The dead would often pay me a visit to recant the days when they were alive, to share memories of times long forgotten...one spirit in particular often came to me when it rained. I remember him whispering to me that the rain reminded him of the day that he and a few scattered members of his village stepped off the boat from St. Domingue and onto the port of New Orleans. He never scared me and over time I grew to look forward to his stories. He would often request that I accompany him on his adventures through the spirit world on a journey back to the port. Hacienda and Camille had both warned me to never accompany a spirit while on the astral plane, at least not until I am old enough and strong enough to bring myself back. They told me that many young witches – the uninitiated to be more specific – have made the fatal mistake of being tricked by a spirit and never woke up.

Just knowing that made falling asleep difficult on many a night. But there were others who would visit me, sometimes begging me to set them free from their graveyard prisons. Camille would sometimes make me a special herbal tea that would help ease my sleep anxiety and then she would draw a protective salt circle around my canopy bed before sealing it with a spell. And for the most part, her magic would work. However, somewhere off in the backdrops of the shadowy underworld, where the spirits of the damned howled for redemption and freedom, where they remained captive to the ultimate slave master, I would hear my name called.

But this night, it was not the young boy from St. Dominque with more stories to share. It was the soft nightingale tone who sought me out. It was the voice of girl, perhaps no older than me who trailed behind the boy from St. Dominique in search of me.

Her voice clung to the gentleness of the light summer breeze that would creep in through my window at night. The whisper of my name would wrap around me like a soft blanket before tightening its grip, packaging me in like the dead wrapped fish sold at the local market. For a while, this voice was an infrequent visitor, stumbling in upon me when I had forgotten about his presence. But the night that followed my discovery of Marguerite Giselle Beauvais, the most feared Priestess/magic woman beyond the Bayou, and my dear mother's plans, her voice grew incessant.

The night of the moon ceremony, after spending most of the night tossing and turning in my bed, visions of a black winged figure reached out to me from the bowels of the earth's crust, beyond the symphony of violent flames, rugged stalagmites, and brimstone. Meanwhile, the voices of the dead grew stronger from the power of the moon and the collaboration of witches, would be witches, shamans, and inexperienced humans, assisted in allowing some of these spirits to pass in between the Veil that separated the physical world from the nonphysical. Tonight, they would dance freely amongst the living and by dawn they would return to the other side of the Veil where they could only observe. This was a time for witches to harness the power of the spirits to strengthen their magic. Tonight, weakened spirits coupled with an even weaker veil would make communication to the spirit world as simple as connecting to the internet. With the energy of the spirits bound to magic, many a witch would be oozing with power. Tonight, would present itself as both dangerous and euphoric for the living and the dead.

It was this particular night I wished I could dance freely, to be anywhere but behind these walls without guilt or shame, like the proud people of New Orleans during Mardi Gras. Many a night like this one, I promised myself that I would one day join the ranks of tourists and locals and take in the magic of the festivities. *One day...* I think to myself as I pull the sheets back over me.

"Hey," came a soft voice that seemed to whisper from the window.

I sit up and look in the direction of the window. Nothing but a breeze filtered through, lifting my white curtains high above the sill, giving a ghastly appearance.

"Who's there?" I whisper, searching the room. "*Ostende te!* (reveal yourself)"

"Do not be afraid little witch," the voice said

softly as it slowly began to take physical form. "My name is Annabelle. I've been watching you from behind the Veil for a while now and I want to help you."

"Help me?"

No sooner had I asked that question, Annabelle sat in the window, her small feet dangling above the floor. She had to be no older than I – nine – and that made me sad.

"Don't feel sad," she told me, her gold hair illuminated under the light of the moon. Her pale skin held an ethereal glow to it, giving her a more "otherworldly" appearance. "It's safe where I am. I'm happy here. One day, I may be allowed another chance at life, but there is no hurry."

"Oh...how did you..." Suddenly, the remainder of the question became trapped in my throat. Death is supposed to be a friend to a witch like me – at least that is what I was taught. And I've spoken to spirits before, but the more I gazed into the pale blue eyes of my new friend, I couldn't see her as a spirit.

"Die?" She chirped, continuing my question. "I was a sacrifice to an old god, a god who preferred the flesh of children."

Even then, regardless of how much death or how close the call of death whispered in my ear; my blood drained from my face making me look paler than her. Annabelle laughed, sounding like the sweet sound of the wind chimes that once hung outside my window.

"That was a long time ago," Annabelle continued. "That's why I said, I am safer here on this side. Humans can be cruel." She studied me with a sort of quiet reverence before making note of my room. "You have a lovely home. You should be happy here."

"I am happy here," I said quickly.

"Even though your wicked mother wants to sacrifice you?"

I looked away. Each day that I lived brought me one step closer to my fate and it seemed as if I was the only person aware of what my mother's plans were for me.

"We don't like her over here," Annabelle added. "None of us do – at least the good spirits. She tells lies and makes promises to those who do follow her, for power and more access to the human world. That's why I want to help you. You are special Maya. Your destiny is greater than just becoming a sacrifice to a dark angel."

"How am I special? My mother is the one with all the power and besides, I was told that the power that I will soon have will destroy everything anyway."

"I am not at liberty to tell you your future, but you are needed Maya. So, think of me as your new best friend. I'm going to help you as much as I can. Just don't tell anyone -not even your coven sisters that you talk to me. Ok?"

I nod just as I hear footsteps approaching my room.

"I gotta go, ok?" Annabelle tells me. "I will be back tomorrow."

I throw the blankets over my head and fight to remain as still as possible. My door creaks open and I can sense that it is my mother who stands in the doorway surveying my room.

"Hmmmm, thought I heard voices in here," she murmurs. "Spirits must be everywhere tonight." She lingers for a few seconds more before closing the door.

I have no idea how long it took before I was able to exhale, but the last thing that I remember before closing my eyes, is a sense of relief...

Maybe, just maybe, things were going to be ok.

SEVEN

The glaring heat of the sun's light poured through the glass of my windowpane and my sweat pulled me from under the heavy cloak of sleep. Normally, my mother would come awaken me to begin my studies at around seven. But after my series of pillows all toppled over onto the floor, while my comforter remained pushed to the very foot of my bed, I pushed myself up and wiped the dried saliva from my face. It took a few seconds for it to register that the alarm clock on my dresser read 8:15.

"Oh!" I gasped as I slid out of the bed. "Dang it. She's going to *kill* me." I swallowed thickly just as the thought exited my mouth. My heart's heavy pounding in my chest and the memory of the dark sinister voice of the ancient demon – the voice of one of the Fallen, Samael to be exact, chilled me to my very essence. However, I could only live in the now and being seated at the table to start my studies was more important than a distant destiny of doom.

It's going to be alright," Annabelle's calm voice whispered in the back of my mind. *You have friends here that want to protect you. Your mother is too exhausted from the spell work she performed last night. Go. Sit. Eat. You will be fine.*

Her reassurance slowed my hurried steps into an even pace as I made my way to the bathroom. I flipped the light on and almost instantly, startled myself upon first glance in the huge mirror that hung above the sink. I looked like a tornado had blown through my room and sucked me up into its vortex. My thick curly mane stood up in all four directions, the straps of my nightgown was twisted above my shoulders, and a thick line of saliva still covered my face. However, I continued to gaze at my reflection, silently making note that my mother and I shared the same pair of eyes; the soft rounded peak on our noses; creamy skin; and a fiery spirit.

But she treated me as if I was nothing more than a tool, a means to complete her work. Nothing more.

Tears filled my eyes as I continued with my morning routine and by the time I was done, I managed to slip out of the bathroom undetected…that is until Hacienda came bursting out of her room.

"Whoa kiddo," she yelped as she jumped back, nearly avoiding a full on collision with me. "Slow down. Where's the fire?"

"I woke up late," I whisper quickly. "I don't want to get in trouble."

"Nah, you won't get in trouble. Your mom is still asleep. Camille is in the kitchen getting started on your breakfast now."

So, Annabelle was right. Thank the ancestors.

"Are you alright? Looks like you had a rough night," Hacienda continued, giving me a head to toe look over.

"I'm fine," I croaked, avoiding her concerned look.

"Did anything spook you last night? The Veil has been thinning for the last few days…did anything come through and bother you?"

I shook my head profusely, determined to keep Annabelle a secret.

"I can tell that you've been crying," Hacienda said, kneeling down to meet me at eye level. "Talk to me."

"It's nothing," I told her.

"Hmmm," Hacienda frowned. "You know you can talk to me, right?"

I nodded but remained steadfast in my silence.

Hacienda sighed. "Well, whenever you are ready to talk, I'm here." She rose to her full 5'5'' height and smiled. "Your powers are coming in. We can all feel it. And I understand how scary that can be. I've got to make a run to the store but when I come back, want to join me outside and see some magic?"

She knew exactly what to say to perk me up. Out of all of my coven sisters, Hacienda could manipulate the elements- also known as earth magic- with her specialty being fire. If she wanted to, she could burn an entire house to the ground and leave no trace of evidence that would point in her direction.

"Yes!"

"Good!" Hacienda chuckled. "Go get some breakfast and...chin up, ok?" She turns around and disappears into the bathroom, leaving me alone in the hallway. The snap, sizzle and pop of bacon interrupted my thoughts, sending a message to my stomach as a reminder that it was time to eat.

"Maya!" Camille called out from the kitchen. "I know you are up! Come to the kitchen!"

"Coming!" I shouted before I darted off in the direction of the kitchen.

———

"Maya," Hacienda said to me a few hours later as we stood underneath the tall tree that had guarded the property for the past two decades. Its branches hung low, gently sweeping the ground during the windy days and I loved it for that.

"Now I need for you to really pay attention. Get still in your mind and listen. I know you can do this," she continued. "Do as I do. Dig your feet into the ground. Imagine yourself a tree, your feet and your legs are like the roots – like that tree over there," she adds pointing back at my favorite tree. "Look at its roots, see how they poke up from the ground before they disappear into the earth. Be the tree. Feel the ground..."

Hacienda sucked in a deep breathe and closed her eyes. I do the same, still pushing my feet deeper into the soft soil as I mimicked her breathing technique.

"Feel the pulse of the earth Maya," Hacienda whispered. "You are a witch, a daughter of the earth herself, a bridge between the living and the dead;

the gateway between the physical and the spirit… allow the earth to connect with you. Feel her heart. Can you feel her heart, Maya?"

Underneath my feet I felt a pulse, a distant beat that sent a gentle vibration through the soles of my feet. My palms warmed and tingled with energy; my heart began to race and the voices… so many voices and languages wrapped around me, pulling me higher, gently lifting my feet from the earth. The voices increased in volume, visions of the earth, the sound of her sweet song of harmony slowly being eaten, ripped apart and consumed by death, disease, and war. The earth is now a prisoner of dark magic, her power slowly being siphoned away by the evil that wrapped its tendrils around her… the evil that has taken refuge within her.

Hacienda is calling me in the distance, but magic that awakened within me felt too good. I could see into the past, the present and even the future. For a second, I saw a girl, a little older than me. She stood strong holding a large silver blade, and in the background, the sky is a mix of blood red and pitch blackness. Who was she?

"Maya!"

My head snapped back as another burst of power passed through me. There was no way for me to stop, even if I wanted to. *I'm finally strong,* I whispered to myself. *Strong enough maybe to stop my —*

"Maya!" Hacienda gripped my leg, using all of her strength to pull me down.

"No!" I screamed, the soundwave from my voice sent her flying backwards into the clothesline. She collapsed in a heap on the grass. Earth, her anger filled me as more voices filtered in and out of my mind.

There you are little one, came the deep ominous voice from deep within the earth's belly. *You are much stronger than I could have imagined. Come to me... set me free so that I may reward you and your bloodline with everlasting power.*

His voice triggered a cold streak of terror through me and without thinking, I waved my hand over the ground beneath me and watched as it splintered into a six foot wide cavern. Panic erupted around me. More voices. My coven sisters rushed outside, chanting, spell casting, using their power to try to seal the huge cavern in the ground that is deepening by the minute. My mother positioned herself in front of me and begins to utter a series of sacred words to close the portal beneath me.

"Let go of the source Maya! It's too much,"

Camille called out. "You are not strong enough to control it."

"Dimittere eam (Release it)!" My mother commanded, her eyes turning jet black. She held out her hand. "Give it to me my child," her tone softer. She inched closer to me with her hand still raised for me to accept. For a moment, the raging fire that burned within me cooled. I imagined myself being pulled into her arms, wrapping myself around her loving protection. But then the anger returned, and the painful memory of her plan resurfaced. Flames of fury danced in my gaze. I could hear the screeches from a legion of demons, clawing their way to the surface.

"Dimittere eam!" My mother's voice cut through the chaos that not only surrounded me but threatened to consume me.

Everything around me stopped. The energy, the power, the rage disappeared, the fire dissipated. My short plummet to the ground felt like I took a dive off a cliff. The last thing I remember before hitting the ground was my mother's look of terror and the sound of Camille calling my name.

CHAPTER

EIGHT

aya! Maya! Wake up! It's not time for you to go yet, Annabelle's voice whispered to me.

But I don't want to wake up, I whimpered back. I just want to stay with you forever.

But you can't stay with me, Annabelle countered. You have a purpose.

I don't want a purpose...

Oh, but you must! You are needed both here on the other side and on earth. So, wake up!

"Maya! Wake up honey," Camille's soft voice coaxed me from my peaceful pool of darkness, the quiet space of my ancestors and the border of the spirit world and back to reality. Surrounded by the comfort of my pillows and embraced by the softness of my bed, I groggily pushed myself up. Hacienda, Camille and of course, the High Priestess – my mother. My other sisters stood back in the other spaces of my room, watching silently.

"What happened?" I managed to ask. My palms still tingled from the effects of the magic that I tapped into.

"Oh, thank God!" Hacienda sighed. "This was all my fault. I shouldn't have tried to teach you earth magic..."

"Earth magic?" I frowned, trying to focus on what happened in the backyard. Slowly the memories returned, beginning with me placing my feet into the dirt and listening to Hacienda's soothing voice as she guided me into a meditation.

"Don't worry yourself about it too hard," Camille said gently. She leaned forward and touched my face.

"You harnessed some really strong juju," Hacienda continued. "Many seasoned witches wouldn't be able to do what you did. And you're only nine."

"My child," my mother began, smoothing a stray hair out of my face. "Phenomenal. Absolutely phenomenal." She shifted her attention to Hacienda, who shrunk back from my mother's gaze. "You will continue to teach her." My mother paused and turned to survey the rest of the room. "All of you. Show her your skills and teach her all she should know. She has demonstrated that it is time for her to prepare for her journey as a witch... it is time."

To my surprise and everyone in the room, my mother leans forward and places a quick kiss on my forehead before springing to her feet. "Everyone back to your routines. Maya needs some time to rest."

One by one each of my coven sisters slowly left the room but not before giving me a kiss on the head or a gentle pat until I was finally alone. "I will be back to check on you in a bit," Hacienda promised as she closed the door behind her. I collapse back in my mountain of pillows.

Learn as much as you can, Annabelle's voice whispered from the ethers. *You are going to need it.*

NINE

His words haunted me even in the dreamscape. Here in my cosmic space of refuge, on the astral plane, where I believed would be the only place for me to escape the call of my bloodline even if for just a little while. I found myself sliding down the rocky surface of a deep cavern. The heat and smoke from the brimstone made it difficult to breathe. The palms of my hands began to blister as the heat that emanated from the stone increased the deeper, I climbed into the cavern. His voice was calling me. I felt the tendrils of his dark energy pulling me downward. My heart pounded against my chest; fear clawed at me. I closed my eyes and tried to remember why I was even down there to begin with.

"Hacienda," I say weakly. "Annabelle...help me."

"Do not be afraid little one," the sultry baritone voice called out to me. *"You and I are friends. I knew you long before you were born my dear, sweet Maya..."*

"Maya wake up!" Annabelle's voice pulls me out of the nightmare and back into reality. My eyes snapped open and instant relief claims me. The early rays of sun peered in through the violet colored curtains that Hacienda had hung for me as part of the décor for my room.

"Annabelle, thank goodness it's you," I exhaled, pushing myself up off the pillow.

"You need someone to do a protection spell on you when you are sleeping. That demon will always find you on the dreamscape." Annabelle regarded me her big blue eyes filled with worry. She patted my head, smoothing the wild strands out of my face.

"I'm not good at spells," I sigh. "Mother says spells are for advanced witches."

"You unlocked a gateway straight to the dark pits," Annabelle shrugged. "I think that makes you advanced."

I plopped back into my pillow and exhale sharply. "I guess so. But its not going to change the fact that my mother is going to sacrifice me to a hell lord."

"We have time," Annabelle declared proudly.

"We have to get you out of here before the eve of your sixteenth birthday and that is only a few years from now."

"How?" I groan. "Everyday that I'm here, I am closer..." I paused, horrified at the direction of my thoughts.

"Try not to think too much about it. You have to stay strong," Annabelle said, her voice becoming a whisper. "I must go. Someone's coming."

Annabelle disappeared into the ethers just moments before my door swung open and in came one of my younger coven sisters Janelle. Her skin always reminded me of the darkest hour before the dawn, its rich midnight hue illuminated the magic that flowed through her veins. Janelle's African lineage could be traced all the way back to the western shores of the ancient lands of Yoruba. Her specialty was Haitian Voodoo magic, just like my mother. The thing is Janelle was chosen by the protector of the *Crossroads* and it was said that it wouldn't be long before she left our coven to start her own. A part of me hoped that if she decided to do so, she would take me with her.

"Grand Rising little Beauvais," she chirped, moving toward my curtains to spread them open.

"Grand Rising Janelle," I murmured, rubbing my eyes. "Where is Camille or Hacienda?"

"They are out in the town to pick up some items for the house. High Priestess will be away most of the day making preparations for a special client of hers and the other sisters will be busy tending to their own duties," Janelle explained. "Which means, I will be teaching you some of the history of the oldest form of magic..." She spun around theatrically; her long locks lifted high above her bare shoulders. Her purple peasant skirt gave her a more radiant appearance. I always wanted to be as beautiful as Janelle.

"Your blood is a combination of all dark magic, which would make you most closely connected to the source," Janelle continued. "But your blood also carries traces of Voodoo, which grants you permission to call on the Loa when you need them."

The last time, I made contact with one of the Loa, it was the Baron who greeted me. Angry doesn't even begin to describe his response. Had it not been for Camile and my mother, I would have probably made an early visit to the grave. But given the way my life was headed; it was becoming evident where I was destined to go.

"The Loa don't like me," I said, recalling the

incident with Baron. "They said I was not welcomed."

"That is because they did not recognize you. Your blood is too strong," Janelle took a seat on the edge of my bed and smiled. "Today they will recognize you as one of their own. And trust me, they will help you. Now get up. We have much work to do."

I told you help was coming, Annabelle whispered to me. *Trust me.*

CHAPTER
TEN

Most covens do not consist of diverse backgrounds of witchcraft. Normally, covens consist of witches who share a preference for a particular practice, for instance Wicca, or ancestral magic. Our coven is unique to most because it consists of witches from all different types of backgrounds and specialties. Even the deities that my sisters work with vary from Papa Legba to Diana, Isis, and other spirits. My mother is one of the few grand witches who is skilled in multiple practices and respected by multiple deities. My mother has enough power to speak to and control demons, but our true power source rests in death magic.

The most powerful witches can harness and manipulate energy from multiple sources – including from that of the deceased. Being that energy never dies but can be transmuted and transformed, the graveyard, sites stained with the blood both the innocent and the damned, are power bases for witches like me and my mother and the other women that lived and died from our bloodline. It fuels us – something that I would not come to understand until many, many years from now.

While Janelle straightened up my room, I rushed down to the kitchen to pour myself a bowl of cereal since Hacienda and Camille were not home to help me with breakfast. This was the first time I would be allowed to work with another coven of sisters other than Hacienda. Janelle also worked more with my mother directly than the others and as I poured the Frosted Flakes into my bowl, a hint of fear crept into my mind: Does Janelle know what my mother plans to do?

She does, Annabelle responded in my mind. I whipped my heard around to see if she had appeared but all I saw was the familiar layout of the kitchen. *But that's why I said help was coming. It is your mother's blood that the Loa do not like which is why they rejected you at first. They sense her evil.*

How are you able to commune with the Loa? I asked, curiously. Voodoo is a closed practice and the spiritual boundaries to this realm are not opened to those who are not descendants of the African slave trade. My mother taught me that much. Witches like my sister Morgana, Camile or even Hacienda are blocked from it and those who dared to summon any one of the Loa would suffer dire consequences. And there is no amount of initiation or even the petitions from strongest practitioner that could change that

I'm an ascended spirit now. It has been many centuries since my own death, and I have visited many realms. I am a good spirit and, on this side, as long as I am an Ascended, I am allowed to at least speak with the other gods and goddesses that I am not spiritually linked to. You and I share a common fate which is why I was sent to help you. A young powerful witch with a huge destiny should not meet Death until she has fulfilled her life's work. And... Samael must never know freedom.

Oh...what if mother finds out that there is a plan to help me?

Do not worry about that. As long as you do not alert her to the fact that you are privy to her plans, you will be safe.

Thank you so much Annabelle! I tried to fight back

tears, tears of relief. As long as I had the support of the spiritual world, Samael will never be able to take me.

Now eat, Annabelle commanded. I must go. There is still so much work to do. Time moves differently here.

"Are you crying Maya?"

My mother's voice startled me, causing me to drop my spoon and some of the cereal on the floor. I turned around to meet her curious expression. She wore her hair tightly wrapped with a red cloth wrap that matched the red caftan that hugged her curvy frame.

"Uh, no I'm ok mother," I reply quickly, wiping my face.

"Are you sure you are alright?" She asked as she approached me. "As of late, I have sensed an alarming amount of free range spirits lurking about, especially near your room. You are not afraid of them, are you?"

I shake my head profusely. "No. They do not wish to harm me. I just…"

"You just what?"

"I just had a nightmare is all," I manage to say. I carry my bowl to the table where I set it down before climbing into the chair.

"Your dreams will become more vivid and

lifelike as your power grows," my mother said evenly. But I can put down a protection spell to act as a barrier for you."

I shake my head again. "Its fine."

"Hmmm..." my mother frowned. "Come see me when you and Janelle are done with your studies for the day."

I stopped chewing. Normally when my mother requests that I see her it means that I am in trouble.

"You are not in trouble," she continues as she regards me calmly. "I just wanted to speak with you about your powers and your experience with earth magic."

"Ok," I croaked, taking a huge spoonful of cereal, and stuffing it into my mouth.

She disappeared up the stairs and it isn't until I hear the last creak of the floorboard above me that I exhale in relief.

Maybe, I can do this, I thought to myself.

"Are you ready Maya?" Janelle called out from upstairs.

I looked down at my bowl and realize that most of my cereal had turned soggy. Camile would kill me for wasting food, but I just could not bring myself to eat it.

"Coming!" I shouted. I quickly hop down and

rush over to the sink where I dump the contents out and rinse away the evidence before making a dash up the stairs.

ELEVEN

Each bedroom in the house is large enough to accommodate a full size private bathroom and is built to ensure each member of our coven privacy. Janelle's bedroom was adjacent to mine; however, it wasn't often that I was allowed in there. Her room was like a fantasy world, it's like walking into another realm. On her walls hung African masks, based on the designs of the Yoruba people from centuries ago. Books on Voodoo including that of New Orleans and its derivatives such as Hoodoo and Santeria – all of which have the same origins – lined her bookshelves that decorated her walls. Incense burned, offering a rich, woodsy scent that cleansed the atmosphere of the room.

Different crystals sat on her nightstand and dressers; a lifelike statue of Oshun sat across from her canopy bed. Jars filled with herbs, dirt and other materials used for magical work.

On the floor is a hand drawn diagram, written in an old language with archaic depictions of deities, most of which I could not recognize.

"Sit," she instructed as she quickly plopped down outside of the boundaries of the diagram. In turn I did as I was told, curious about today's lesson in magic.

"As a witch with the power to pass through the Veil," she began, 'it is important that I teach you about the magic of the Crossroads: the space between life and death; your physical body and your spiritual form; the space where Ashe is hidden, where all magick resides. You have the power to unlock the forgotten and the forsaken...which makes you very special."

Her smile always put me at ease, and I leaned over to further inspect the drawing. "My magic scares me," I confessed. "Is that the reason why I can't play with the other kids?"

My question surprises her and she opens her arms, motioning for me to take a seat on her lap. She folds me into her embrace and hugs me. "It is hard being what we are. Born with gifts and power that normal humans would never understand is hard – for all of us, but it is especially harder for children. I was like you once," she said as she continued to rock me in her arms. "I was too powerful for my own good. The Loa respected me and granted me every request I made; they protected me and my family from our enemies and they even guided me to this coven where I can protect witches like you." She paused as if she caught herself for a mistake in saying more than what she should have. "You have to remain sheltered until you are able to control your power. You are not safe in a world that will not understand you – at least not yet."

"I understand," I whimper. I've always understood why I could not go outside and play hopscotch with the other girls who ran and danced and played in the neighborhood. I also knew that our neighbors were mostly afraid of us, especially of my mother. I heard the whispers; I saw the stares and I knew about some of my mother's acts of petty vengeance on innocent but recklessly nosy spectators. It just was what it was; however, it still didn't stop the loneliness or the need to connect to someone my age.

"A soul with that much power is an old one,"

Janelle continued with a chuckle, "which is how I know you understand. Now let's get started...In order to properly understand Voodoo, you have to know who the Orishas are– divine spirits that help humans navigate our daily lives. They are the sons and daughters of Olorun, who is the Supreme God, the Creator of all things. These divine have all laid the groundwork of Voodoo magic as we know it."

We spent the morning and well into the afternoon reviewing the differences between Haitian Voodoo and New Orleans Voodoo – which is the spark that me and my mother are most connected to. She even taught me which offerings were best to give to both Papa Legba and the Baron and how to tell the difference between the two. We ended with Janelle placing a protective marker with blessed ink at the base of my wrist and giving me instructions on how to move forward with accessing my Ase` from the crossroads.

"Do it tonight. Papa Legba waits for you to meet him at the Crossroads," she said sternly. "Whenever you are in trouble with your magic Maya, go to the Crossroads."

I walked out of Janelle's room feeling empowered and even more hopeful about my future.

But even then, I did not realize the power of Janelle's words returning to me until a few years later when it was almost too late.

TWELVE

Your mother is waiting for you, Annabelle whispered to me as I took my time down the dreaded corridor towards my mother's room.

I know, I think back to her. *I'm scared. What if she knows that I know what she is going to do to me?*

She doesn't...at least not yet. Stay calm. I cannot go in there with you because she will sense me.

Ok. Come to my room when I am done, ok?

You bet. You can do this Maya!

Annabelle's voice disappeared the moment my hand reached for the doorknob. Smoke filtered into the hallway from one of her altars that she kept lit. I spotted the outline of several spirits who walked to and fro from her doorway and throughout the house. Her door swung open, and I carefully crossed over the threshold and into her room.

"You don't have to be afraid dear daughter," she smiled. Mother was seated on the edge of her bed, going through a stack of paperwork, which was a bit strange considering she spent most of her time summoning, conjuring, and managing the coven. "How did things go with Janelle?"

"It was ok," I shrugged.

"It was *ok*?" My mother chuckled. "Just, ok? Surely, you were as amazed with Janelle's skill and knowledge as you are with Hacienda's earth magic?"

"I am. It's all just a lot to remember," I breathed.

"I understand. It's different than working with the elements. You will master it in time." She paused. "Tell me, how did it feel to open up the gates?"

I look away and tried to focus on Annabelle's soothing spirit. The last thing I wanted to do was revisit those terrifying moments when I felt the presence of the same dark entity who demanded that I become a living sacrifice to his freedom.

"It was scary," I confessed.

"And what else?" Her tone remained even and calm, but I knew underneath it was a cold demand for an answer.

"I felt the Darkness," I continue. "It was hard to breathe…there was too much power taking over me. I thought I was going to die."

"But you didn't," my mother said proudly.

"I thought I was going to hurt everyone too," I add.

"Oh, you know your mother was there

to protect you and the others." She paused again and looked at me, her expression solemn. "You do know that right? I will always protect my coven, but especially you."

Her words brought tears to my eyes. I wanted so badly to believe that my mother, Marguerite Beauvais, had truly loved me like any other mother would. But even then, I had already accepted the fact that my mother loved magic and power more than her own daughter; and given what we are and the power that came with our bloodline, "normal" would never reside in our vocabulary.

She pulled me to her bosom and cradled me, like she used to do when I was smaller. I inhaled her scent; she always smelled like fresh Gardenias. "My sweet Maya," she cooed. "You have so much power for being so young." She continued to rock me, humming old lullabies that she used to sing to me until a soft rap on the door interrupted her.

"Come in!" My mother called out after she released me. She kissed me on the head and pushed me off the bed.

Morgana slowly stepped inside, eyeing us curiously before offering me a smile. "High Priestess," she said. "We have a fanged visitor."

"A vampire?" I asked, my eyes wide with excitement. "A real one?"

My mother frowned. "He must have a death wish," she said evenly. "Maya, remain upstairs. Vampires are incredibly dangerous, and some are even quite powerful."

"He's an Old One. Hacienda and Janelle have him contained."

My mother sighed and quickly rose to her feet. "I will deal with him."

"Are you going to stake him?" I blurted out, capturing the attention of both Morgana and my mother. "I saw it on TV. In order to kill a vampire, you have to put a stake through his heart."

Morgana chuckled nervously while my mother regarded me with a smile. "As a witch, there are a thousand different ways for us to kill a vampire without having to resort to using a stake." She then kneeled down and took my hand in hers. "Keep up with your studies and I just might show you one night how a witch takes care of those disgusting night feeders." She stood up and led Morgana out of the room with me following behind them.

"Stay upstairs," my mother commanded. With a wave of her hand, she willed me back to my room and sealed the door with an invisible barrier.

"Dang it!" I fuss out loud. "My one chance to see a real vampire...gone!"

"Finally!" Annabelle gasped as she appeared from the ethers. "I started to worry about you."

"There is a *vampire* in the house," I tell her excitedly.

Annabelle turned her nose up and frowned. "Eeeewww...no entity in any realm wants anything to do with them."

"I know they freak me out too," I said. "But still, I want to see what they look like in person. I heard that vampires are made from old magic."

"Vampires are the result of an ancient curse," Annabelle continued. "But we have plenty of time to talk about that. First, listen to what I have to tell you. It's definitely something you should know..."

CHAPTER

THIRTEEN

"Your Uncle Kevin is on his way here to try to rescue you," Anabelle told me.

I didn't know much about my Uncle Kevin other than the fact that he and my mother never got along and that he used his magic for healing people. My mother always said that Uncle Kevin was jealous of her but if I'm being honest, I never saw that from him. The few times when he did come around to visit, he was kind to me.

"How do you know?"

"He's been communing with the spirit world for assistance," she shrugged. "Some of the spirits are petitioning for assistance on his behalf."

"Seriously?"

"Yes." She paused, her curious blue eyes studying me.

"When is he coming?"

"Soon, I guess... just keep in mind that when he comes, say nothing about your mother's plans."

"But if he is going to rescue me then he should know what she is going to do," I protested.

"He already knows. That's why he is asking for help. But the less people who know that you know, the better. There is a greater plan at work here. We can't mess this up."

Hurried footsteps from the hallway quickly began to close in. Annabelle and I glanced at each other. "Gotta go. Remember what I said," Annabelle whispered as she faded away.

"Maya!" Hacienda called out from behind the door. "Are you alright in there?"

"Yes!"

Hacienda pushed the door open, her curly mane levitating off her shoulders. "High Priestess sent me up here to keep an eye on you. Every available witch in this coven is on guard. An Old One is here."

I looked up at Hacienda, her entire five foot seven frame crackled with magic. "I don't understand why we have to do business with them.

He shouldn't even be allowed to set foot over the threshold."

"What's an Old One?" I asked, curiously.

"A vampire that is over five hundred years old," Hacienda grit through her teeth. "They are stronger than Masters, who are over the age of one hundred but under five hundred and even harder to kill – regardless of how strong of a witch you are."

"My mother can take care of him," I said, trying to sound hopeful.

"She can...that I have no doubt. But he could still take some of us out before she even gets a chance to rip his black heart from his chest." Hacienda marched over to my window and pushed the curtain back. "I hate vampires."

A low growl reverberated throughout the house, instantly capturing Hacienda's attention towards the door.

"Shit," Hacienda cursed. "I think there are more of them."

"*Esse abiit daemonium!* (Be gone demon!)" Janelle's voice rang throughout the hall.

"*Praesidio carmine!* (Protection spell!)" Camille shouted, running up the stairs. She burst into my room, her magic igniting a red-orange flame on both of her hands. "We are surrounded. Whatever business High Priestess has with that demon-"

Filias coniungere magicae! Ejecti vetus. Ego mittitur eius mortuus anima in flammis mortis. (My daughters join your magic! Cast out the old one. I will cast his dead soul into the flames of death.) My mother's voice echoed into our minds, her call to action. Without thinking, I stretched out my mind to connect with hers and through her eyes I saw her pinned to the wall, the vampire's grip on her wrists were like steel bolts pressed against the wall, his fangs just inches above her neck.

"Witches like you always think you have the upper hand just because you can summon a few low level demons," he growled in her ear.

A gust of wind blew in through the house, breaking the windows. I could feel my mother's power rise like an invisible tide. Her dark rage blew open every closed door, shattered glass and we could hear the screams of a few of the vampires that waited outside in the shadows.

"Quick! Grab hands! The power of three!" Camille commanded as she reached for my hand.

"The power of Four–" Morgana said as she rushed in.

"Five–" Came Janelle.

I felt my sisters take my hands and I could hear their chants, calling forth protection from the spirits and connecting their magic to strengthen the barrier. But my mother, we were still connected. Her fury became my own and my head snapped back. I broke free of the circle that my sisters had formed and from my own palms a dark energy which I directed to the ground.

"*Spiritus ex supra voco super vos* (Spirits from beyond I call upon you)! *Auxilium mater mea* (Help my mother!)!"

The floor beneath turned jet black, forming a pool of dark murky water in which one by one, hundreds of demons spewed from. Their screams were nearly deafening. My sister's fear coated the air like a heavy paint on dry wood.

"We do not serve Marguerite," they hissed in an ominous tone. "Let alone a child."

"You will *obey* your master," Janelle growled as she stepped forward. "Or I will bind you to the fatty body of a boar where you will suffer until the day you are slaughtered."

The demons released a collective hiss. I could feel my mother's heart beating faster. With her mind she willed the broken shards of glass into the shape of a dagger while the vampire cackled with laughter.

"*Si obedieritis mihi.* (You will obey me.)," I continued. "*Ego, Maya Beauvais, filia Summus Sacerdos praecipio tibi Legionem, ut serviant mihi. Nisi mater mea a faucibus damnati*! (I, Maya Beauvais, daughter of the High Priestess command you Legion to serve me. Save my mother from the jaws of the damned)."

The demons released a loud pitched scream. In my mind I could see the Old One had paused, curious to know the direction of the noise. My army of demons took flight in the direction of my mother's room, becoming a black blur of smoke. The temporary distraction allowed my mother enough time to send the shards of glass into the center of the Old Ones back. He screamed and snarled, back handing my mother hard enough to knock her off the wall. My demon army surrounded him as he thrashed about, struggling to pull the shards of glass from his back. And just as quickly as they surrounded him, they engulfed him in flames.

My mother stumbled, still dazed but strong enough to utter the words, "*Frigidus,*" instantly putting out the flames, leaving nothing but a gelled puddle of ash. The demons disappeared, returning into the hidden underbelly of hell. The connection with my mother dropped too and I could no longer remain on my feet. The last thing I remember as Hacienda called out my name was the familiar voice in my head applauding me.

"Well done, Maya," he said. *"Well done."*

FOURTEEN

"*Do not be afraid of me Maya. I am here to help you,*" *Samael whispered from the darkness. "You are powerful, more powerful than your mother. The world needs to be prepared for someone of your power..."*

"*What do you want with me?*"

The darkness around us began to tremble; the surrounding heat began to thicken and off in the distance I could hear in the distance the painful wails of the damned echoing from the deeper pits of the abys.

"*Accept your fate Maya... You. Are. Mine!*"

"Maya!" Annabelle interrupted; her hazy worried expression came into view as my eyes fluttered open.

"Not again," I whined, grabbing my pillow and

covering my face with it. "I passed out again, didn't I?"

"Do you remember any of it?" Annabelle asked, her face still just inches away from mine.

"Some of it," I admit, sifting through my recent memories. I saw myself tap into the darker spaces of myself where my magic resides. I heard the voices of the demons that I summoned to do my bidding. And then I remembered that vampire who held my mother hostage, threatening to siphon her life force. I could've ended it then. I could have allowed her to die by his hand and I would have been free of her and her promise to Samael.

"It is not her time, and it is not your fate to spill her blood," Annabelle said softly. "You have a greater destiny at stake."

"It doesn't feel like it," I sighed.

"I keep telling you Maya," Annabelle huffed. "You have to trust in the greater good – your destiny."

"How do you know that it is all just going to work out?" I asked, suddenly feeling defeated. "Look at what happened to you? Do you think that you are being sacrificed to a demon lord was part of the 'greater good'?"

Annabelle looked away, her pain becoming my

own as I am instantly filled with regret. "I'm sorry," I said quickly. "I didn't mean to say that."

"No, no... it's fine. I don't even miss my human days anymore," Annabelle replied, pushing her long strands of gold hair from her face. "But before I can answer your question, let me show you something...."

She reached for my hand and pulled me forward. "Sit up. Open up a channel so I can show you what life was like for me then..."

She pressed her forehead against mine and together we closed our eyes. When our minds merged, we found ourselves in the center of a busy market square.

"Where are we?" I asked, looking around. Several large men wearing bright colored tunics idly strolled by, excitedly engaging in a debate in a language I did not understand. They smiled at Annabelle as they passed by.

"Home," she grinned. "This is Macedonia... where I grew up."

Large monoliths of stone structures that were prayer temples attracted people by the droves. I looked around, amazed by the colorful garb that adorned the bodies of each mysterious passerby who made their way to the temple.

"There are so many people," I gasped, taking a look around. "Why are we here?"

Annabelle offered a sad smile. "Follow me. Today is a very special day." She took my hand and guided me through the crowd.

The midday heat quickly began to take a toll, and although Louisiana temperatures were not for the faint of heart, but here in the year 900 BC, the terrain offered a different level of extreme heat. We pushed past a small group of men unloading goods and herbs from the backs of their camels.

"Come on," Annabelle urged, leading us to the front of the gathering towards the flight of stairs that seemed to go on forever. We came to a stop at the bottom of the stairway, as the crowd behind us gathered, with more people trailing closely in the rear. Annabelle's gaze remained fixed at the top of the stairs; her gaze haunted by the figure that approached. Tears filled her eyes as she watched the hooded figure become flanked by two men who smiled at the crowd. On the far right of the platform where the three of them stood was a pyre built from stacks of cedar wood and stone. I realized then by what Annabelle meant when she said this was a special day.

Horror claimed me as we looked on at Annabelle being led to the pyre. One of the men, turned to face the crowd with a smile before removing Annabelle's hood.

"This was the day that they set me free," she whispered, her gaze focused on the pyre. "I was chosen to be the virgin sacrifice to a demon god. My people believed sacrificing me would protect them from what was to come. But they were wrong..."

The two men guided Annabelle to the pyre and carefully lifted her up to gently stretch her out onto the pyre. Both men worked effortlessly to secure her hands and her ankles as the crowd watched.

"We don't have to stay," I whispered to her. "I understand now."

Annabelle said nothing, she just continued to relive the horrific events that took place centuries ago directly across from us atop the stairway. I covered my face with my hands as tears began to blur my vision. The crowd began to cheer when a younger female, a child perhaps no older than I, approached the pyre carefully holding a lit torch.

No, I thought to myself as sudden awareness settled in. "Annabelle, we can leave now. I don't want to see anymore."

"You have to see...understand my truth and my pain so that you will know why your future is so important," Annabelle whispered. "I had gifts just like you do. I wanted to use them to help my people. If I had been allowed to live, I would have been powerful enough to

stop what was to come...but, they signed their own death warrant the moment the flames consumed my body."

The entire crowd fell silent the moment the child passed the torch to the elder who stood quietly by the pyre.

"If you are wondering Maya, if I felt the pain as the fire tore into my flesh," Annabelle continued. "I didn't. I had taken a tonic the night before which rendered me numb to the fire. I didn't even feel the earth beneath my feet when I was led to the platform. Nothing could have been more painful than the fact that it was my own father who lit the pyre and watched me burn for the sake of a deity that did nothing but wreak havoc and destruction amongst my people."

FIFTEEN

Annabelle released me from the vision and together we released a hard exhale. Unspent tears continued to blur my vision as I wrapped myself in the mountain of blankets that covered my bed. If my mother is successful in sacrificing me, her blooded daughter to the Fallen, would I become a lost spirit like Annabelle? Forever wandering the realms as a child with no direction towards ascension.

"I do not ascend because I choose not to," Annabelle answered. "Many powerful witches were sacrificed or threatened to be sacrificed, to appease the gods of men. These gods change faces and purposes like men change shoes. I hope to become a guardian angel one day and in order to do so, I need to save as many of you as I can before I can get my wings."

Her last comment made me smile. I could only imagine what Annabelle would be like as an angel, her gold hair already created a halo around the top of her head. Her innocent green eyes were filled with so much love and compassion that it might have been possible for her to have been an angel in the flesh during her days as a human. "You already are an angel," I said to her.

Her red rimmed eyes quickly lit up as she leaned forward to embrace me. "Thank you, Maya," she sniffled. "That means more to me than you can imagine."

"You will always be my guardian angel," I whisper to her. "Always."

"Maya!" Hacienda called my name from the corridor, reminding me and Annabelle that it was time for her to depart. "I will be back later. I sense trouble coming, so stay alert," she said quickly before disappearing.

"Coming!" I yell at the door.

"Are you dressed?" Hacienda asked as her footsteps became closer. "I thought you would be up already."

"Ummm..."

The door swings open and in came Hacienda, her gaze sweeping the room, searching for another presence. She paused and glanced at me curiously. "Uh, Maya?"

"Yes?"

"Was there someone else in here?"

Don't lie, don't lie, don't lie, don't lie... "Who else would it be?" I asked, careful to maintain an even tone, lest one wrong inflection would cause her to raise an eyebrow.

"If you are communing with spirits Maya, that's fine," Hacienda began. "But please be careful. There are entities that wish to harm young witches like yourself."

"I know," I shrug.

"Good. I need you to get dressed. We have a guest that is coming by today," she announced.

"Who is it?" I ask as I slid off the bed.

"Your uncle," Hacienda replied evenly. She moved quickly into my room and began searching through my drawers, looking for an outfit for me to wear. "And Maya?"

"Hmmm?"

"Please be on your best behavior today," Hacienda continued as she pulled out a yellow short sleeved blouse that had a butterfly in the center and a powder blue spaghetti string top. "Things are a bit tense right now between the High Priestess and your Uncle Kevin."

"But why? They are siblings."

Hacienda sighed. "Differences in opinion, I suppose. Your Uncle is a strong Shaman, which is indeed quite noble. He operates on the 'light' side of magic, while your mother and witches like myself would be considered to be on the darker side of the magical spectrum."

"I thought magic was neither good nor bad," I add, looking down at the two shirts Hacienda had picked out for me to decide on. "I want to wear the blue one," I declared proudly.

"Fine, albeit the yellow one would look great with the jean shorts Camille bought for you." Hacienda reached down into the last drawer to search for the final touches to the outfit. "You are true and correct, Maya. Magic is neither good nor bad. It's all energy and it just depends on the intentions, or better yet the will of the user. You can either be born with the power to wield magic or, if one is a mundane human, you usurp that power from demons, or form an alliance with an entity which ultimately places that human under the dominion of something else. That's the great thing about being a witch Maya, we are *born* to hold dominion over the spiritual. Nothing holds power over us..."

I could think of one particular demon that holds power over all of us. Even my mother, the most powerful Grand Witch in all of Louisiana was under the control of something even greater than herself. And considering who this particular entity is, I would gladly accept the option of being a regular human any day.

"It's going to be extra warm today, so that blue camisole and skirt fits the weather perfectly," Hacienda chirped.

"Can I go outside today and play with the other kids?" I asked. Tension in my body began to build as Hacienda considered my question.

"I mean, I don't have a problem with it. You need to be around other kids," Hacienda shrugged. "But High Priestess gave strict orders about you doing so. I mean, kid, you are ridiculously powerful, and we don't want you to accidentally hurt one of the human children."

Quiet defeat once again plagued me. There was just no way for me to have some freedom away from all of the witch stuff.

"But," Hacienda continued. "I will ask your mom

if it would be alright for you to hang with some of the neighborhood kids and I will even offer to supervise. Just remember that you can't use magic to help you win a game of kick ball. That would not be fair."

I couldn't remember the last time since I smiled the way that I did in that moment. Normally, my days were spent locked in the house, surrounded by adults who talked about demons, spirits and magic all day. It had been since forever I would be allowed to join the other kids in a game of hopscotch or jump rope. I peered around Hacienda's slender frame outside and I could already hear the other kids gathering on the corner. I couldn't wait. Maybe, this will also prevent me from inadvertently ruining my future survival since I will be too busy playing outside to fall under the influence of my Uncle Kevin.

And for a little while, I could pretend to just be normal.

Good job, Annabelle whispered to me. Playing with the other kids is a great diversion tactic. One of the girls, you will know her by her single blue eye, she will help you too.

"C'mon," Hacienda motioned for me to follow her. "Let's grab something to eat before it starts to get really busy in here. We have a few new clients that are coming in, on top of Kevin's impromptu visit...and I need to speak with your mom before she gets too preoccupied with running this place."

"Do you think the other kids will like me?" I asked, taking Hacienda's hand as she led us towards the kitchen.

"What's not to like?" Hacienda beamed as she looked down at me. "But hold your horse's kid. Let me get the ok from your mom. I'm just as excited to release you into the wild as you are to go."

"She's going to say yes," I declare firmly. "Just watch. You will see."

"Well, you are a strong psychic too so, I'm betting on you kid."

SIXTEEN

"You know how I feel about her interacting with the human children," I overheard my mother say to Hacienda as I crouched just outside her bedroom door. "Especially now with her magic being as strong as it is."

"I know but she's still a kid ya know?"

Please don't give up now Hacienda, I silently plead to myself. *She's going to say yes.*

"She is no ordinary child Hacienda. My daughter has the potential to level an entire neighborhood or better yet unleash an army of demons onto unsuspecting humans – not saying that I am entirely against that idea – but not a risk that I am willing to take."

"Just for two hours," Hacienda continued. "Two

hours of her running outside, burning off that energy, and allowing her to adjust to the magic or frequency of the sun. I will watch her. I don't have any clients to attend to today and besides this will give you and the rest of our coven 'child free' space. "

Even from behind the door I could feel the harshness of my mother's hard gaze burning a hole right through poor Hacienda. *I should have never asked,* I scold myself.

Relax, Annabelle whispered to me. *It will all work out.*

"And just *where* will my child be running around at?" My mother demanded.

"I see the kids normally convening right across the street at old man Mulligan's house to meet up with his grandkids," Hacienda continued, her voice unwavering. "Then they head on over to the park which is right around the corner – walking distance."

"How old are these kids?"

"Somewhere between eight and twelve. On occasion, one of them will ask about Maya. I mean, they've seen her around and probably want to know why she doesn't come out and play or isn't allowed to come out and play. I usually just tell them that she is busy with her studies – which is true."

The silence that followed was so unnerving, my stomach tied itself into knots. My palms began to sweat, and I felt like I would spontaneously combust from the pressure. After what felt like a painful eternity of suspenseful waiting, my heart skipped several beats when I finally overheard my mother say, "Fine."

Yes! Without thinking I quietly do a victory skip into the air. *She almost never says yes.*

I told you. There is a plan for Maya that is at stake.

"If anything happens Hacienda, and I do mean *anything,* you will face the hand of my wrath. And not even your ancestral magic will be able to protect you. Am I clear?"

"Crystal." Hacienda replied coolly.

"Good. See to it that Maya at least finishes her chores before she goes outside."

"Will do High Priestess..."

I back away from the door to give room for Hacienda to exit and held my breathe as she closed the door behind her. I watched as she tilted her head back and released a hard exhale.

"Alright, go clean up your room. It's still early so maybe we can beat the kids to the park and no magic kid. Ok?"

"I know. No magic. Thank you so much Hacienda!"

"You are welcome. Now let's go before High Priestess changes her mind."

"Remember what I said kiddo, no magic. No talking to spirits. No channeling. Just focus on having fun. We only have a couple of hours so make the most of it."

"Ok," I said uneasily as I eyed the group of kids that had gathered near the swings.

"I'm going to sit right here underneath this big tree," Hacienda said as she spread out the blanket that was folded and tucked neatly under her arm.

"Ok," I said again, this time making eye contact with a girl who couldn't be any older than myself. She smiled and waved, which captured the attention of the other seven children who were gathered around with her.

"See? They are already welcoming you," Hacienda said, offering a supportive smile. "You have nothing to fear but fear itself."

"But I don't want to hurt them," I whispered, as I looked back at Hacienda.

"You won't. Now go."

Reluctantly I took one step forward, my heart beating against my chest, and my palms clammy, and I kept going until I reached the swings. The girl with the auburn hair, warm smile and the one blue eye and one green eye approached me. *So, this is the girl,* I think to myself. *Annabelle was right.*

"Hi," she said meekly. "I'm Willow."

"My name is Maya," I said, keeping my eyes focused on the ground.

"You live in that spooky mansion across the street from my grandfather's house, right?" Asked an older boy, with dirty blonde hair and even dirtier overalls.

"Hey, that's not nice," Another girl scolded.

"Well, it's true," the boy argued. "We were told to never go over there and especially to never walk in their yard otherwise they would turn us into a bag of bones."

I cringed at his condemnation and suddenly, I just wanted to go home. Maybe my mother was right after all. This was no place for a girl like me.

"Don't listen to him," Willow said gently. "He's just mad because his grandfather has old people disease and is crazy. Nobody listens to him."

"Ay, you shut up you!"

"Don't tell her to shut up Willard!" Came another girl who stood an inch shorter than Willard, with hair as fiery as the words that flew out of her mouth.

"Get out of my face Nancy," he growled, stepping away from her.

"Well say sorry," Nancy continued, placing her hands on her narrow hips. "Say sorry or I will punch you in the face."

Willard looked at me, his dark eyes still filled with contempt. "Sorry."

Willow shook her head at Willard and gently took my hand. "Come on, lets walk over to the pond." She then lowered her voice and said, "Annabelle sent me. I'm just like you. My mother is part of a Celtic coven not far from here."

"Please don't tell the other covens about me," I plead. "I don't want them to cause trouble with my mother."

"They won't. Most of them don't want trouble with your mother. She is too powerful."

"Oh...ok."

"Are the others like us?" I asked, still keeping my voice low.

"No. They are just regular humans." Willow paused as if she were waiting for the others to catch up. "Last one to the pond is an ugly frog!" Her laughter ignited a flame of joy – a feeling that was relatively unfamiliar to me and for the first time, I felt like a kid. Not a witch with a powerful destiny, but a kid.

"Hey!" I shouted running behind her at full speed. "Wait up!"

SEVENTEEN

We laughed. We jumped. We danced around in the grass, made up songs using our names. Willard eventually came around and engaged in a round of tag with me. Nancy even introduced me to the other kids, aside from Nancy and Willard (who already made their introductions): Whitney, Jonathan, Lucy, and Britney. Nancy and Whitney pulled out two thick bands of long rope and taught me how to play "double-dutch" which involves jump roping with two ropes instead of one. We were so busy laughing and playing that I did not realize how much time had passed and when I saw Hacienda tapping her watch, my heart sank.

"I have to go you guys," I sadly told the group.

"Awww but we were having fun," Jonathan groaned.

"Don't act like you don't have parents," Nancy scolded him before giving him a hard nudge.

"Do you think you can come back tomorrow?" Willow asked. *Send me a signal,* she thought to me.

I don't know how, I told her, surprised at the strength of her telepathy.

Send the message through Annabelle. We can communicate that way, ok?

Ok.

"Is that your mom?" Willard asked, pointing at the quickly approaching Hacienda.

"Uh, no, she's – she's my aunt," I stuttered.

"Are you ready Maya?" Hacienda asked. "Your uncle is waiting for you back at the house."

"Yeah," I tell her. "I'm ready."

"I will bring her back," Hacienda promised the group.

"Can we come to your house?" Willard asked. Nancy sighed and offered him a hard punch in the arm.

"Can you please for one second, not be stupid?" She demanded, with her hands on her narrow hips.

"One day Nancy, I'm going to pop you a good one!" Willard threatened. "I swear I am."

"Hey no swearing," Hacienda chuckled. "Listen, let's take it one day at a time. You guys are out of school until when?"

"Next week," Willard answered proudly. "I'm an A student by the way."

"Well good for you kid," Hacienda chirped. "Keep up the good work. Maya will be back to hang with you guys another time. I promise."

"Bye Maya."

"–Bye Maya..."

"–Bye!"

"Bye everyone!" I waved before turning around with Hacienda to exit the park.

"You had fun kid?"

"I did!" I chirped with a burst of energy. "Thank you so much Hacienda!" Without thinking I do a quick skip and twirl in the air. For the first time ever, I felt what its like to be free: free of magic and destiny. It was then I realized that I wanted to be more than just the daughter of a powerful High Priestess. I wanted to be Maya.

"Well, I'm glad you had a good time."

"Do you really think we will be able to come back again?" I asked.

"I don't really see why not," Hacienda shrugged. "No magic, no problems. We survived."

I turned around one last time to watch as my group of friends continued running and laughing near the swings. The urge to snatch away from Hacienda and run back to them grew stronger, however, I continued my walk with Hacienda back to the house. The last thing any of us needed was Hacienda to pay the price for my disobedience.

My Uncle Kevin stood on the front porch with an herbal cigar settled between his fingers, as his gaze drifted between the white fencing that was in desperate need of repainting, and the weeds that grew out between the thorny bushes of roses. When he spotted us, his normal indecipherable expression shifted to excitement.

"Well, there's my favorite niece!" He belted out proudly. "Come on over here and give your uncle a hug!"

It was rare for me to see my uncle; but the few times that he did come around, I could never hide the fact that I was just as excited to see him as he was me. He was a breath of fresh air and a barrier when it came to dealing with my mother. He made me feel safe and proud to be a witch and he understood me in ways that the other members of my coven simply could not.

"Uncle Kevin!" I rushed over to him and welcomed his warm embrace.

"Maya!" He grinned as he scooped me up. "You've gotten to be so big! How old are you?"

"Nine."

"You are a big girl!"

"And she's incredibly smart," Hacienda added as she approached us.

"And strong too..." Kevin said, looking me over. "Her magic is radiating all through me."

"Did you just get here?" Hacienda asked.

"Yeah. I know...I can see that you guys are..." He glanced at the door in time to frown at the older gentleman being escorted out by Morgana towards the fence.

"Busy," Uncle Kevin grumbled. "This is no place for a child you know."

"My name's not Bennit and I'm not in it," Hacienda replied quickly.

"And this is no place for the judgmental eyes of jealous family members," my mother said from behind. She slipped out of the front door; her arms tightly folded against her chest.

"Well, if it isn't the whore of Babylon herself," Kevin griped as he set me back down.

The tension between my mother and my uncle was as thick as a brick wall. I nervously took refuge behind Hacienda as my mother's dark gaze narrowed in the direction of my uncle.

"For what reason would the winds of absolute failure blow you from the dusty trails of Arizona to grand ol' New Orleans," my mother spat.

"I need some help with a spell," he said evenly.

"Of course," My mother replied slyly. "Among other things..."

"Marguerite," Kevin began, taking a step closer towards my mother. "You already know what I'm here for."

"I do and dear brother, I would implore you to think twice about what you might do. There aren't enough ancestors on your father's side to rescue you from my power – you know this."

"This is no place for a child Marguerite. If you want to dabble with the dark arts, then that is *your* choice. Maya has nothing to do with your thirst for power."

"And what are you going to do when she accidentally opens up the gates of hell Kevin?" My mother quizzed. "Tell me. When she summons a legion of demons to do her bidding simply because they recognize her blood signature as dominion, then what? Save me your judgement especially when you know absolutely nothing."

"I know a lot more than you think," Kevin challenged. "I know that you have plans on-"

"Silentium! (Silence)" my mother bellowed, her voice sounding like the thunderous combination of a thousand voices at once. With a wave of her hand, my uncle's mouth was stitched shut, the black string that sealed his lips shut covered in some of his blood.

My scream temporarily distracted my mother from continuing whatever spell she was concocting. It freed Kevin from the binding work, releasing the strings that were magically sewn into his lips.

"*Hinc et numquam redire. Nos sunt sanguinis, non magis.* (Leave here and never return. We are of blood no more)," my mother chanted. Bale strength winds picked up and began to circulate the house. The ancient shamanic inscriptions that lined his forearms ignited. His eyes turned a neon green as he began his own magical chant. I could feel myself being physically pulled in Kevin's direction, and Hacienda quickly took my hands and began to fight against the pull.

Kevin struck my mother with a long, magical cord, which lacerated her skin like a whip. My mother countered his attack with a dark rope which wrapped around his muscular frame.

"Stop!" I called out to both of them. "You don't have to fight!"

The illuminated outline of a large wolf stepped out of the ether and bit through the rope that bound my uncle. Once freed, it turned around to face my mother, the threat of its growl permeated the air. With her will, my mother broke the broom that rested against one of the pillars that supported the roof in half and directed it towards the center of my uncle's chest.

"Nooooo!" With my own mind, I stopped it midair, but only long enough for my uncle to move out of the way.

"*Ego, mitte te ad Compitum...ut Barron choro in-* (I banish you to the Crossroads...may the Barron dance on your-)", my mother began to chant.

"No!" I yell, yanking myself free of Hacienda and rushing over to stand in front of Kevin. "*Ego intercedere in fortitudine mea incruentus. Non erit pulsus ad Compitum. Ipse erit libero hoc carmine et numquam redire hic. Ipse manebit incolumi a te Marguerite Giselle Beauvais. Semper et in aeternum.* (I intercede on the strength of my bloodline. He will not be banished to the Crossroads. He will be free of this spell and will never return here. He will remain unharmed from you Marguerite Giselle Beauvais. Always and forever.).”

The wolf disappeared, as did the black rope and the neon green cord. The makeshift stake dropped onto the porch.

“This isn't over Marguerite,” my uncle growled as he slowly began his retreat towards his black Volkswagen. “This isn't over.”

My mother kept her dark gaze fixed on her brother until he slid into the driver's seat and turned the ignition on.

“It never is,” mother whispered while the three of us looked on as he backed out into the street and sped off.

We stood in silence for what felt like an eternity, before my mother retreated into the house without another word. When she disappeared behind the door, Hacienda looked down at me and said, “Come on kid, let's go inside. I think we've both had enough for one day.”

I fought back my tears and struggled to block out the chain of events that took place on the front porch from my mind. My mother was willing to kill her own brother to protect her secret. The only string of hope I was able to cling to was Annabelle's promise that help was on its way. But the question that remained was from who? Who would be strong enough to stop my mother and pull me out of this twisted fate of sacrifice and death?

EIGHTEEN

The day my Uncle Kevin and my mother battled each other on the front porch of our coven home, was the last day that I would see him for several years to come. None of my coven sisters spoke about that day, not even Hacienda. My mother continued with her daily routines as if nothing ever happened; as if, her own brother did not exist. Surprisingly though, she still allowed me trips to the park, provided I continued to study under the guidance of my sisters. It was my mother's wish for me to focus on Voodoo rather than elemental magic or earth magic; and as a result, I began to spend less time with Hacienda.

Business had also picked up exponentially and nearly every week, our coven hosted parties every weekend, especially before and after Mardi Gras. Men and women from all walks of life, came to the House of Beauvais for mystery, excitement and magic. Morgana specialized in tarot and past life readings; while Janelle offered assistance in root work, divination and conjuring's; Brielle for her skills in death magic and revenge spells; Beatrice for her workings with the ancestral realm and love spells; Camille for her elemental and powerful defensive magic; Hacienda's earth magic, curses and binding spells; and finally, the all- powerful Marguerite Beauvais herself. There were other services that my coven sisters provided, but only for the high money paying rollers who were looking for more than just a stroke of luck or spell work.

There were many a night I awakened to the strange grunts and growls that echoed into the hallways from some of the men who frequented our coven; and sometimes, if I woke up earlier than expected, I've witnessed a couple of overnight guests, tiptoeing out of the front door.

"These men have secrets," Annabelle whispered to me one early morning. *"Be sure to put down a protective barrier every night. Ask Janelle or Camille to help you with it."*

"What's wrong?" I asked. *"Are these men dangerous?"*

"Most of them come here to be entertained by adults –your coven sisters- but there is one who is aware of your presence. He wishes to visit you in your room one night."

My eyes widened and a hard knot began to form in the pit of my stomach. *What does he look like?*

Shaggy brown hair; a long crooked nose and an uneven smile. He prefers the company of children, Annabelle said to me uneasily. *You have plenty of entities to call on to help you too. I am always watching over you.*

Shouldn't I tell my coven sisters – or my mother? I asked as I started to panic. I did not fully understand what Annabelle meant when she said that he "prefers the company of children," but I could sense that it wasn't good. If anything, the dark tendrils of depravity wrapped themselves around me at the thought. The energy was sinister, and I began to consider the benefits of running away.

But where to?

I am shielded from them. They can sense the presence of my spirit, but they are unable to identify me for many reasons – one of those reasons being to protect you. The year and the time are quickly approaching for the gates to open, giving Samael the opportunity to escape.

I don't want to be here anymore... I confess. Everyday that I wake up, I'm scared.

I know and I wish this didn't have to be your story, but you are destined for great things Maya. Put a protection spell over your room every night. If you ever have to leave your room in the middle of the night, I will be right there to watch over you. I will warn you when he is around. Your guardian Loa is Papa Legba. You can even call on the Baron – just like how Janelle taught you.

Ok...

When Annabelle's voice disappeared, I became overwhelmed by the crushing reality of how alone I was. Granted, Hacienda and Camille were always there for me whenever I needed them. And of course, when Annabelle was around, it didn't always feel so bad because she was a kid just like me. The only other person who could really relate to me was Willow, but whenever we met up at the park, we could not talk about "witch things" or about our covens in front of the other kids. Periodically, she would send me a telepathic message to show me some of the moon rituals her coven was teaching her. I wanted so badly to show her my magic, but given the strength of my power surges, the last thing I wanted to do was hurt her.

Plus, I had the sneaking suspicion that my mother would know.

"Maya, are you ready?" Janelle asked as she rounded the corner and entered the kitchen. She stood in the doorway and patiently waited for me to slide down from the tall wooden chair.

"Yeah. I'm ready," I said, mustering a smile.

"Alright... it won't be too long today. I have a busy schedule lined up with several clients."

"Do you think Hacienda will be home today to take me to the park?" I asked, feeling hopeful.

"No. I'm afraid not. Mistress has her out on a special assignment. She should be home soon. But come along. We've only got a couple of hours."

The rest of my day was spent helping my other coven sisters move things around in the house as my mother prepared for the night's entertainment. Special protective barriers were put down around our outdoor perimeter as word had spread quickly throughout the quarters that Marguerite Beauvais had become a household name and that alone also put us at risk of drawing the unwanted attention of other dark covens and entities that wish to harm us.

By the time everything was done, and the daytime clients had finally left the house, I was exhausted.

My spirits were instantly lifted the moment the front door swung open, and the familiar greasy scent of charbroiled meat entered the foyer. Morgana strolled in; her smile wide with paper bags with Pete's signature cartoon logo of the owner's face. She had bought me a burger meal from the world famous fast food restaurant that had served the people of New Orleans for twenty years.

"I don't understand how any of you could eat that wretched meat," my mother scoffed when she noticed Morgana coming in with the bag. "That food is terrible."

To my mother's dismay, me and Morgana loved it. I scarfed down the burger and the fries without shame.

"Slow down, Maya," Morgana giggled. "You might choke."

But I didn't. I had not eaten much all day and Pete's signature aroma permeated the room and was an instant reminder that the PB&J sandwich I had for lunch had run its course.

Once I showered and climbed into bed, Annabelle's warning completely slipped my mind. As I nestled underneath the sheets, the loud jazz music blaring in the background, my thoughts drifted to my days spent at the park with Willow, Nancy, Lucy and the others. It wasn't long before I was completely out, phasing in and out of every world the dreamscape has to offer...until I heard the latch turn on my door and the shadowy form of a thinly built man slipped in between the folds of darkness.

"I've been waiting for this..." he whispered. "Don't be afraid. I'm here to just play with you little girl. Do you want to play a game?"

NINETEEN

He quietly slipped into my room and closed the door. My heart began to race as I remained frozen underneath the sheets on my bed. I could see his shadowy outline inching closer to me, courtesy of the light of the streetlamp that stood as a night sentinel across from my house. His thoughts melted into my mind; those sick and perverted fantasies bombarded my thoughts, intensifying the fear but even worse, making me sick to my stomach. His dark chamber of secrets was filled with the terror and humiliation from many other kids he victimized. The stench of his sins began to overwhelm my psyche. Annabelle's voice called out to me, beating back the painful cries of his victims.

Call him! Call Papa Legba Now!

The tips of my fingers crackled with a concentrated dark light as visions of the interdimensional realm known as purgatory, the space between life and death; the crossroads of ascension and the space where all ashe` - magic – and all of its cycles of creation and destruction are formed. There he sat; his expression grim; his normally almond colored eyes ignited with a yellow light. His waist length locs were decorated with bits and pieces of skull and bone while his dark skin was painted over with the ashes of the deceased. He raised his head and smiled in my direction, motioning for me to approach him.

I did as I was asked, despite the fact that the human male, was slowly closing in on me on my bed. My bed dipped from his weight, and I curled tightly into myself, fighting to remain focused on the vision.

"Daughter of mine," the deity's voice echoed in my mind. "Your Ashe is powerful. One day you will join the ranks of the Loa. Danger surrounds you little one as your blood calls forth great enemies that wish to steal your Ashe." He paused, his eyes shifting from yellow to black. "Interloper! Wicked man! Who dares to violate a living temple of *Ashe*?!"

"Please help me," I whimpered, my eyes filling with tears.

"*He. Will. Die.*" Papa Legba growled. He quickly rose to his full seven foot height, his long locks trailing against the dirt road as he rushed towards me. With a gentle nudge against my forehead, he jettisoned me out of the vision and back into reality, to meet the sinister stare of the rapist. However, just as I opened my mouth to scream, a strike of lightening flashed inside my room and Papa Legba's bulky, menacing form materialized next to my window.

The man paused and turned to meet the now tangible threat of one of the most elusive entities in the spiritual realm. Not everyone who calls on Papa Legba receives an answer. And sometimes, one might call on Papa Legba only to hear the harsh cackle of The Barron. Panic erupted in the household; I could hear the heavy and quick footsteps of my coven sisters rushing towards my room. Annabelle appeared next to me and took my hand.

Papa Legba approached the bed and reached for the terrified man who attempted to spring from my bed to the floor as a means of escape. My door swung open, with Janelle and Camille rushing in, followed by my mother and the others. Papa Legba yanked the man by his foot and dangled him like he was a piece of fruit on a string, his head inches away from the floor.

"You reek of filth," Papa Legba growled.

"Wait! No! Who are you! What are you people?!" The man screamed, tears streaming down his face.

"There is a special someone that I would like for you to meet," Papa Legba said evenly. "As a protector of children, she would be interested to understand your predilections for ..." The Crossroads Guardian looked at me and then back at his victim and scowled. "You disgust me." As he turned around to leave, the man still screaming and struggling to break free of his grip, the Guardian quickly surveyed the room. My coven sisters and my mother fell eerily quiet as his hard gaze bounced between Janelle and then my mother.

"This is a whore house," he declared. "Vermin like this," he continued, giving the man's body a hard shake as an emphasis, "Would have no place here had this...this brothel been a sanctuary for the gifted. The price for my presence will be heavy. My name will not be defiled here."

Janelle lowed her head and said nothing, while my mother however, remained impassive.

Papa Legba's gaze darkened as he regarded my mother. "There is no place for you at the Crossroads; may your blood be your enemy."

My mother's eyes narrowed as she watched the entity disappear with the man in tow. His screams echoed long after he was dragged away into the other dimensions. A period of silence followed as each member of my mother's coven came into awareness of the danger, I was recently in. Janelle and Camille both covered their mouths in shock, the sharpness of their gasps triggered another round of fear within me. I wrapped my blankets around me and burst into tears.

"Maya," Camille cried as she rounded the bed. "Oh my God! I'm so sorry... "

"That fucking bastard," Janelle hissed. "I thought he'd left... Had I known..."

"Maya baby, are you alright?" My mother asked as she stepped forward. "He didn't touch you, did he?"

I shook my head profusely but the terror and the rage that followed could not be undone. My body trembled so hard that my bed began to shake and both Camille and Janelle climbed into the bed with me and wrapped their arms around me.

"He- he climbed into the bed with me," I

stammered through thick tears. "I-I didn't know what to do... so I called..."

"Papa Legba came to your rescue, child," my mother said gently. "You called on someone bigger than you and all of us really to protect yourself. You did the right thing." She paused and looked around the room, her eyes fell on the lone shoe that the man had left behind. "I will see to it that this never happens again. Ever. I will personally screen each and every client and for those with sexual deviances that involve those of a nonconsenting age, will be sent home with a curse that will filter throughout their entire bloodline among other things."

"I'm so sorry Maya," Janelle whispered tearfully over my head.

You did good Maya, Annabelle said softly in my mind. I told you everything is going to be ok.

However, in the days that would follow, as much as I wanted to believe Annabelle's kind words, I held the sneaking suspicion that things would get far worse before everything was ok. And when I made a quick glance in my mother's direction, her dark expression told me everything I needed to know.

CHAPTER

TWENTY

I t had been a few weeks after that frightful incident when Hacienda finally returned home; and during that period of her absence, my mother no longer allowed me trips to the park. Instead, I was confined to the walls of the ten bedroom estate, permitted to go outside only when it related to practicing spell work and magic. My mother also increased the barrier spell around the perimeter of the home, making it difficult for me to communicate with Willow through telepathy. Sometimes her messages would come in distorted, or I could barely hear her voice as it attempted to filter through my mother's barriers. After a while, Willow's voice soon disappeared; and my sole companion became Annabelle.

"Hey kid," Hacienda chirped as she opened the door to my room. "I missed you. How've you been?"

I looked up from my table of dolls and smiled. "Hacienda! You're back!"

"Did I miss anything?" She asked as she entered, dropping her hobo bag on the floor.

I rushed over to her and wrapped my arms around her waist feeling both a rush of excitement and relief. "Where have you been?"

"I suppose you can say with some family I hadn't seen in a long time...and of course, I had to do some stuff for the High Priestess," she shrugged as she hugged me. 'But the important thing is, I am back now."

"I'm so happy that you're back," I told her. "It's been soooo boring..."

"I bet," Hacienda chuckled. "What's with the intense protective barrier around the house?" She asked. "I felt like I had to fight my way in."

I quickly explained to Hacienda all of the strange events that took place in the house, starting with Papa Legba. Hacienda plopped down on the edge of my bed and sat in quiet disbelief when I finished updating her on everything.

"*The* Papa Legba, Guardian of the Crossroads came to your rescue?" She breathed.

"Yeah."

"You've got some strong juju kid," Hacienda added. "Do you know how many of his worshippers, his children of worship would kill to have him step out of his domain to speak with them?" She paused before continuing with her thought. "I'm glad that he got that creep off of you. Some of us weren't so lucky…"

I didn't exactly understand what she meant then, but from the sadness that showed in her eyes, it didn't dawn on me until years later that Hacienda and other witches like her were victims of abuse. Sometimes those traumatic experiences are what activates a witch's power.

"Anyways kid, I'm glad that you're alright," Hacienda said as she stood up, moved quickly towards the door to close it before securing the latch. With a wave of her hand, she surrounded us with her own barrier of magic, its luminescent glow reminding me of the soft light of the firefly.

"I didn't know you could do this," I whispered in awe.

"There is a lot that you don't know about me, kid," Hacienda spoke rapidly. "But listen, I don't have much time left here. And I wanted to tell you before things start to get a little crazy."

"What do you mean?" I looked up at her face, searching for answers. Worry settled into my bones, and I began to panic, hoping that Hacienda did not intend on leaving me forever. I needed her here with me.

"A lot more people – good people- know about you Maya," Hacienda explained. "And they want to help, kind of like your Uncle Kevin tried to."

Does Hacienda know? I think to myself.

"You have a power that someone wants to use for themself," Hacienda said evenly. "I'm not about to allow that to happen. Not on my watch."

"Hacienda...these same people... do they know?" I asked meekly.

"Know about what exactly..."

I sucked in a deep breath and gathered as much courage as I could before speaking. "Samael."

Hacienda's wide eyed expression filled me with immediate regret. *I should have listened to Annabelle*, I thought to myself. *I spilled the beans too soon.*

"I know. They know. The message has already been sent," Hacienda confessed. "I don't know how you found out about that – but considering your powers kid, it is no surprise. But tell no one and I do mean NO ONE. Not even Camille, got it?"

I nodded my head profusely as Hacienda

wrapped her arms around me. "I gotta go. I have more work to do."

The luminescent shield dropped around us and reluctantly, I slid away from her hold. "Ok."

I sadly watched as she grabbed her bag and made her way to her room.

It's happening, Annabelle said as she took form in the center of my room.

As much as I wanted to smile and greet Annabelle with some form of excitement, a deep sense of dread filled my stomach. The level of betrayal that Hacienda would perform against my mother would only mean one sure thing: a lot of people would get hurt – including Hacienda. Whoever was coming to help, needed to be prepared to fight not an ordinary witch, but a witch with the power to call forth hell.

TWENTY-ONE

"Maya!" My mother called out to me the next morning as I was quietly pilfering the cabinet for Hacienda's secret but not so secret stash of cupcakes. My head popped up like a chipmunk from its burrow caught red handed with my loot.

"Coming!" I said, my heart pumping anxiety and nervousness into my veins. I quickly closed the cabinet and raced up the stairs into my mother's chambers where I found her seated calmly on top of her blood red duvet. The Golden Girls playing softly in the background. She offered me a quick smile and motioned for me to close the door.

"Janelle says that you are doing well in your Voodoo studies – which is pretty obvious considering our most recent visitor," she began. "I know I don't say this often, but I am quite proud of you. You are advancing faster than I was when I was your age."

"Thanks ma- uh, High Priestess," I said, feeling slightly uneasy. It was rare for me to find her looking about as ordinary as a normal human. No candles were being burned. The musky scent of incense had disappeared.

"I may be the High Priestess, but I am still your mother," she said. "I know sometimes it doesn't feel that way and you do spend most of your time with Hacienda..." She then cleared her throat and focused her gaze on me. A small part of me wanted to dart out of the room and hide in one of the many hidden cabinets scattered throughout the house. "Whenever a witch shields herself or enacts some sort of protective shield within the cover of these walls, I always know. There are many things that go on underneath this roof, most of which your sisters are not aware that I am privy to. I know that Hacienda was speaking with you when she shielded herself with her magic...what did she tell you?"

My eyes dropped to the floor as I nervously began to rub my hands together unsure of what to say. Annabelle could not appear in the backdrop of my mind to offer assistance. *What do I say?* I think to myself. I struggled to summon calm when there was none. If she knew what Hacienda was up to or the plan that was to unfold, I could only imagine the dark, twisted punishment that she would enact on my coven sister. However, Hacienda was more than just my coven sister and mentor, she was my friend.

"I know that you love Hacienda," my mother continued, her tone softening. "We all do. She is an incredible and powerful witch – a valuable member of this coven. I just wanted to know if she is in trouble. I cannot protect our household if I am in the dark about the danger that lurks in every corner…"

"She's not in trouble," I began slowly. "I had asked her where she had gone… I didn't mean to get her in trouble!"

"Now, now Maya, no one is in trouble," my mother said coolly. "Now please, tell me… where did Hacienda go?"

I swallowed thickly and tried my best to walk that fine line between the truth and a full out lie. "She went to visit some friends and…" I lowered my voice. "She said she went to do some stuff for you…"

"Ah yes, she did not fail me by returning empty handed," my mother commented. "And those friends of hers…are they of another coven?"

I shook my head profusely, still avoiding her hard stare.

"Hmm, well it doesn't seem like much of a conversation that needed to be shielded," she added.

"I told her about what happened that night..."

My mother raised her eyebrow and inhaled slowly. "Go on... "

"I told her about what happened at the Crossroads..."

"And what happened at the Crossroads Maya? You didn't tell me about that."

"Papa Legba said I was going to become a Loa someday."

She paused and studied me curiously, her gaze becoming more vacant with each passing second. "I was called to be the next Loa for our bloodline," she said softly. "At least that is what my mother – your grandmother told me. I spent my childhood training to become all that I am today only for me and the women that came before me to be banished from that realm – even in death."

It was then our eyes met and the truth – her dark truth revealed the reason for her accepting the Dark Oath, to become an Enchantress of Death. Her soul would have no place in any realm, and should she meet her end, her soul would just end up as food for the very demons that she held dominion over. There would be no ascension for her or an opportunity to walk amongst the Guardians of the many realms. Her fate would be far worse than death itself.

And my mother would do whatever she needed to do to ensure her own survival – even if it would cost me my own.

I stood in front of her for several minutes, unsure if she truly bought my story and would go no further in investigating Hacienda. I trembled at the thought of her using her psychic abilities to pry my mind open like a can of ravioli to seek out the truth about me and Hacienda's conversation. But she didn't.

Instead, she offered a weak smile and said," You can go on Maya. That was all I wanted to know."

It took a few seconds for it to register in my mind that she had released me. Once outside her door, I scurried as quickly as I could to my room and closed the door behind me. Annabelle materialized shortly after; her eyes lit with excitement.

"Phew that was close!" She chirped. "I'm so proud of you for staying strong!"

"Shhhh, we have to be quiet," I spoke in a hurried whisper. "My mother has eyes everywhere. She can *hear* everything."

"I am protected by white light magic," Annabelle declared proudly. "She cannot fully penetrate that power. Remember?"

"Yeah... I guess..."

"Cheer up. I have a message from Willow for you."

"Really? Is she ok?"

"She's fine. But take my hands and open up your mind. This is important."

TWENTY-TWO

I did as she requested, both anxious and excited to hear what Willow had to tell me. Despite Annabelle being an apparition or better yet a spirit, her hands felt oddly soft with a hint of warmth.

"I'm stronger now," Annabelle breathed with her eyes closed. "Close your eyes. Link your mind with mine."

A distorted image of Willow's small frame appeared in my mind's eye. She stood in the middle of the park, by the old tire swing, wringing her tiny hands together. "Maya," she began, fighting back tears. "I won't be able to visit with you anymore. My coven – we are in danger."

My heart dropped and I almost broke the connection to Annabelle, but she held on tightly. "Don't worry," Annabelle soothed. "Keep watching."

"Your mother has declared war on all covens in the French Quarter and all of Louisiana. We don't have that kind of power to defend ourselves against her magic. My mother said it is no longer safe for me to communicate with you anymore. She said that Marguerite would be sure to find us if I continue to talk to you."

"Wait, no!" I screamed in my mind. "How could she do such a thing?"

"There is a war that is happening around us Maya with the other witches. They are afraid of Marguerite's power. Our community has been divided – there are those who wish to stand against her and there are those who just want peace. My family wants peace and the freedom to practice the white magic of our ancestors. We don't have the power to fight Marguerite. She will kill us all."

"Maybe I can stop her," I whispered hoarsely.

"You can't stop her," Willow said sadly. "None of us can. There are powerful witches out there that may be able to help but we have to find them." Willow paused, wiping her face before she continued. "I wish I could say more and maybe one day when we are older, we can be friends again. I will find you again Maya. I promise. But right now, I have to go. But don't lose hope. More friends are coming...and one more thing."

"I don't want to hear anymore Annabelle," I whimpered. "Please."

"No," Annabelle said gently. "Please, just listen."

"There is a girl that is about your age and special like you," Willow told me. "She has powers and is destined to protect humanity from the dangers that threaten to destroy all of us. She will need you and several others soon because the fate of the world is in the sword that she will carry. That is all. Don't do anything crazy or stupid Maya." She smiled before her image disappeared.

I snatched my hands away from Annabelle and dropped to my knees, unable to fight the tears that rained down from my eyes onto the floor. Another person who wanted to love me, to be my friend, had to exit my life because of the doings of my mother. When will any of this end?

"Maybe it will be better for everyone when I am dead," I cried. "Everyone I love leaves me because of *her*."

"I will never leave you or forsake you Maya," Annabelle vowed as she crouched down to wipe my face. "I will be here with you until the very end. But like I always tell you, worry not. Willow revealed to you a vision – and one of great importance. Have I let you down yet?"

"No," I sniffled.

"Good." Annabelle paused and glanced over my shoulder. "Someone's coming!" She faded away, as I scrambled to wipe my face and smooth my hair back. The door swung open and in came Camille, with a small wooden bowl in her hand.

"Maya, have you seen my..." She stopped mid-sentence; her brown eyes filled with worry. "What happened?" She rushed over towards me and gathered me in her arms.

"Nothing. I'm fine," I said. "Really."

"You were crying. What happened?"

"Nothing. Nothing happened. It just..." I released a frustrated sigh. "It really sucks being a witch sometimes," I blurted out. "I can't have friends. I can't do what regular girls my age can do. I just hate it!"

"Maya..."

"I just want to be left alone for a little while," I told her, suddenly feeling exhausted.

"Alright," Camile relented, sounding defeated. "I will give you your space...but I'm here when you are ready to talk."

She released me and as soon as the door closed behind her, I simply crawled into my bed and wept.

TWENTY-THREE

I spent most of the afternoon alone with my dolls, trying to distract myself from my thoughts. I hoped that Willow and her family were safe, that they've gotten as far away as possible from New Orleans and the entire state of Louisiana. I wondered how the rest of the gang was, Nancy, Willard, Lucy; Whitney; Jonathan; Britney... with Willow gone, did they still meet up at the park? I hadn't heard their cheerful and boisterous laughter for a few days, as they would parade down the street, but I had reasoned that it was because they had returned to school. Now, it was easy for me to guess that Willow had been the glue that held them together.

And now all that I had left was a few scattered

memories of my days at the park, when I could just be Maya, not the cursed daughter of Marguerite Beauvais, the most powerful dark witch in Louisiana.

"Your mother has declared war on all covens in the French Quarter and all of Louisiana..." Willows words filtered into my thoughts, on repeat like a broken record in the depths of my mind. Since birth, I was taught that witches, sisters of magic, weavers of the thin fabric of life that grounds us to this planet and gatekeepers of the spiritual world were supposed to be united. Even those who worked with the darker realms rarely feuded with each other for the simple fact that each one of us held the potential to destroy the balance of the physical realm.

But my mother was never one to obey rules – even the rules that she herself created.

I have to do something, I thought to myself. *I have to stop whatever it is my mother intends on doing. I have to protect my sisters.*

The large hand sewn doll that Camille made for me seemed to stare back at me in agreement. The doll was made in my image, with fuzzy black yarn sewn onto its head to represent my messy, thick coils. It was embedded with protection magic so that I might always feel safe.

A soft knock on the door interrupted my thoughts. "Maya?" Hacienda pushed the door open and came inside. "Maya, are you alright? Camille said you've been locked in your room all day."

I looked up, my eyes once again welling with tears. However, before I could respond, the mind numbing headache that marked my mother's psychic summon forced me on my back and Hacienda to her knees. The pain could only be best described as the worst migraine headache mixed in with a utility drill digging deep into the center of one's skull. I opened my mouth to scream but no words or sound could escape it all remained trapped in my throat, locked in my vocal cords as I struggled to even breathe.

"There has got to be a better way for your mother to call us," Hacienda groaned, her hands gripping both sides of her head.

The attack lifted almost as quickly as it began and for a few minutes, the only thing that either of us could do was remain, unmoving where we were. My head still throbbed; however, Annabelle's gentle spirit quietly wrapped her hands around my head and slowly siphoned away the pain.

Convene to the front room in five minutes, my mother's voice followed.

Hacienda carefully pushed herself off the ground. "This has to be serious if she called you too," she grumbled.

The sinking feeling in my stomach told me that it was more than serious...the lives of every witch in the house was on the line.

I sat between Hacienda and Camille on the love seat while the others were scattered throughout the room with my mother standing front row center. Her palms crackled with magic as dark as her fury which she trailed into the room. Her thick curly hair which she normally kept piled high and wrapped above her head, hung loosely, past her shoulders.

"The time has come when those who would dare challenge our power would reveal themselves," my mother stated, her gaze bouncing from each of us. "Thanks to the information that Hacienda returned to me, magical contenders have invaded our territory and intend on usurping our land to feed their thirst for power. I will not stand for it."

"They've already begun psychic attacks on Morgana," Janelle added, offering her a supportive glance.

"They have also been sending spirits to spy on us which would explain a lot of the ghostly activity that has been happening as of late," my mother added dryly. "They've been testing our boundaries, our limits and looking for a source of power greater than their own – and they found it." She took a moment to examine our expressions before focusing on me. "There has been a lot of supernatural activity as we all know, courtesy of the thinning of the Veil and more and more humans attempting to access power that they could never understand."

As my mother continued to rally my sisters, encouraging them to use their gifts for warfare against the other witches, I quickly glanced over at Hacienda's stoic expression and wondered if she knew about the many covens who lived in fear of my mother's power. I wondered if she too wanted to put a stop to this; to protect those whose magic was unmatched to my mothers.

"It's the House of Brixa," my mother seethed between clenched teeth. "I will have Minerva's heart on a dinner plate and serve it to their bastard children." My mother's dark glance returned to me. "All of you will assist in defending this coven – even you Maya. With Maya's abilities, we will have the strength of a thousand powerful witches, which is more than enough leverage if you ask me."

Nooooo, I screamed in my mind. I looked around at my coven sisters, unsure of what it was I that I was hoping to find in their expressions, but whatever it was, it wasn't there.

Get ready kid, Hacienda whispered to me in her thoughts. *When the time comes, run and do not look back.*

TWENTY-FOUR

"Samael, I beseech you for assistance," I overheard my mother's channeled whisper. The urge to creep to her room and lean my ear against the door to listen grew strong. However, even then, the strength of my intuition held me in place, and I focused my energy on listening from a distance.

"You wish to wage war with the others?" His deep voice boomed from the ethers. "And why is that? Are you not powerful enough? Have I not granted you and members of your coven enough?"

"Yes. But this particular coven has been snooping around, rallying the other witches against me. I suspect that they are even aware of my precious Maya...if anyone learns of her power and future potential, they will attempt to take her from me...from us."

"I see..." Samael grumbled; his voice trailed off as he were contemplating her complaint. "You are the most powerful sorceress in the Quarter – and perhaps in the entire world. There hasn't been a witch of your magnitude for centuries."

"But there are those who wish to usurp my power, to channel what is in my blood for their own gain. I will not have it."

"Those who you seek to destroy have also been loyal followers of mine. Their offerings have granted me strength, strength in ways that you alone cannot bring me...that is, until Maya is given over to me."

"If my enemies are successful in their pursuit of my destruction, then the promise of Maya's blood to undo your shackles will be forfeited. And it may be another thousand years before there is another opportunity for your release from your prison in Hell."

"Fine. But consider this my last act of mercy upon you Marguerite Beauvais. I have waited patiently for my due and–"

"The eve of her sixteenth birthday, she will be properly cleansed and offered to you as promised. Her blood will set you free and you will reign as Lord of this earth realm for all eternity," my mother promised.

Samael released a soft chuckle. "Good. I look forward to it. Do what you must then Marguerite."

I slid against the wall onto the floor, gripping the doll that Camile made for me against my chest. A soft whimper escaped my mouth and tears filled my eyes. Regardless of what Annabelle or Hacienda said, there was no way out of this. I was born to be a sacrifice to a Fallen One. My death would mean the destruction of humankind just as much as my birth. Innocent people were going to die and there would be nothing I could do to stop it.

***

We all convened once again in the front room, surrounding my mother in a protective circle, hand in hand. Over a red, lit candle, my mother spoke in an ominous tone as she lifted a small dagger above wrist, before digging deep into her flesh.

"*Ortum, ex cinere reconditum in tenebris spatia meum sanguinem, patres mei tenebris magicae* (Rise, from the ashes hidden away in the dark spaces of my blood, my ancestors of dark magic); *Dicere porro omnis pythonissam de singulis angulo bayou* (Call forth every witch of each corner of the bayou). *Perducat nos ad terras, ubi defunctorum requiem* (Bring us to the lands where the dead rest). *Commoda mihi potentiam tuam, passurum fluunt per me. Probare nobis quod Domus de Beauvais tua fide.* (Lend me your power, allow it to flow through me. Prove to us that the House of Beauvais has your loyalty)."

Gale strength winds burst through our windows, leaving trails of shattered glass in its wake as it surrounded us. I gripped Bria and Morgana's hands tightly and squeezed my eyes shut, wishing that I could be at the park again, laughing and chasing Willow and her friends around with a stray dandelion that I'd found in some made up, round about game of tag. In my mind I heard Willard's voice, accusing of us of cheating when I touched him with the flower. I saw Nancy, with her hands pressed on her waist scowling at Willard. I saw Hacienda's warm aura under the rays of the sun, as she rested next to the neighboring Oak tree.

I felt the flame of the candle grow in heat and intensity until it stretched forward towards all of us, licking away at our skin. I was the only to cry out in pain and terror. I fought against Morgana and Bria's hold to break the circle, to escape the agony of the flame that stripped me of a small piece of my flesh as if it were taking an offering.

"No! I don't want to do this!" I wailed against the wind and building fumes. "I don't want to do this! Somebody help me!"

But it seemed as if my voice fell upon the ears of only the truly dead. Even Annabelle, my spirit guide remained silent as I shrieked with horror. My lungs burned from the smoke and my forearm bled from where the fire burned me. As I remained bound to my sisters and my mother focused on the center of a powerfully dark spell, I could not connect to my own power and on some level, I knew that none of us could. Our powers were completely null and void for as long as the dark spirits of magic held us captive through my mother's spell.

The ground beneath us rumbled and shook, but my sisters remained steadfast in their determination to not break our circle- a supposed representation of our bond and our magic. For a millimeter of a second, my eyes snapped open, and I could see nothing. The smoke blotted out every opportunity for light to filter through, leaving us incased in total darkness. As the ground continued to shake, I felt the shift in the air from us being transported to the center of St. Mary's cemetery. It was here that I not only had to stand face to face with some of the darkest covens I would ever come across. And worst of all, not only were we outnumbered but those of us who possessed dark power would be at peak magic right at the beginning of tonight's full moon.

With the sun having disappeared, revealing the shadowy outlines of the thickets and ferns that lined the cemetery's walkways, I could not be certain if the fight would begin before the moon reached its peak or after. As we stepped out of the smoke to meet the hard glares of the women who deemed our coven enemy number one, a few of them flinched in surprise when they made note of my presence.

Don't worry, Annabelle's voice whispered to me. *I'm right here. I brought some friends too. Just do whatever I say, got it?*

TWENTY-FIVE

"You would dare bring a *child* to a fight?" Said a woman with dark hair that she pulled to the side, allowing it to cascade over her shoulder. She coolly approached us, her hands massaging a red apple that I detected to be a tool used to channel her power. "There are those of us who are willing to completely abandon all forms of morality for the sake of the craft, but..." Her gaze softened as she looked at me. "Even this is a new low."

"Well how can you call yourself a dark witch, a mistress of darkness, if you are afraid to go to Hell?" my mother countered.

"Marguerite, you will pay for the atrocities you have committed against our coven," she continued.

"Several of my girls could not even receive an immediate burial as we had to go through extreme means of undoing the spell work that ravaged their bodies."

"Well, Brixa, if the newly initiated cannot withstand a simple spell, then why were they initiated? Using inexperienced baby witches to spy on someone of my standing is sending them to their death."

The other women who stood behind Brixa grumbled their collective hatred for our coven, the dry leaves rustled underneath their feet, making me feel more unedge. I clung to Camille's skirt; her gentle hand rested reassuringly on the top of my head.

"You dragged us all out here from the comfort of our homes to do what exactly?" Brixa demanded as she shifted the apple from one hand to the other.

"It seems like she wants to have a pissing contest," one of Brixa's witches sneered from the back.

I looked up at my mother in time to see her eyes turn jet black. The whispers of our ancestral spirits turned to shrieks. A thick, heavy root tore through the ground beneath us, disrupting and destroying several of the old tombs that surrounded us before ripping through the dirt and winding itself around Brixa like a giant serpent. Brixa's shout was quickly silenced when a thin vine coiled around her face, circling over her mouth.

I shut my eyes as the thick root squeezed Brixa until her bones snapped like twigs; until the blood curdling scream broke free from her lips; until her eyes burst from their sockets; and until her screams could be heard no more. My eyes snapped open when Camille ushered me behind her as the sky darkened and the thirty plus gathering of enemy witches all moved at once, disbursing various forms of magic in our direction.

"Praesidio! (Protection)", Camille shouted with a wave of her hand. She motioned an invisible shield over us which protected us from a concentrated orb of dark fire. "Maya, run!" She called out, pushing me forward. "Seek cover!"

"No!" My mother hissed, snatching me away.

"Nooooo!" I yelled, pulling back. I used what strength I could muster and successfully slipped out of my mother's grip. "Hacienda! Hacienda!"

"You dare call on another as if she were your mother?" Her gasp cut through the darkness. "You insolent child! You will come to me this instant."

"She can't even control her own child," one of

the witches cackled, trailing behind me. "Come here little girl. I don't bite."

She reached down and touched a thick growth of vines that stretched out from over the tombs and transformed them into several large snakes. I released a high-pitched scream and turned around, running as fast as I could in the shadows. I ducked just in time to avoid a lightening strike. Someone grabbed me from behind, swinging me around in the direction of the chaos. I screamed again, this time however, my fear and anger combined created a sonic boom, which sent us flying in every direction.

Annabelle appeared just in time to soften my blow against the monolithic statue of St. Mary. I stumbled as I struggled to jump back on my feet and Annabelle calmly lifted me up. She motioned for me to remain quiet and then she pointed in the direction near the main entrance of the cemetery.

Five black sedans lined the street as several heavily armed men and women, carrying protective gear preparing to take position around the entire site. More screams echoed in the darkness. From the corner of my eye, I witnessed a blonde haired witch use her kinetic power to drive the sharp end of a broken tree branch into the center of Morgana's chest.

No! Morgana!

My feet take off before my thoughts could fully register what happened. My heart was filled with grief. This has to stop.

Maya! Come back! Annabelle's voice wrapped around me and stopped me mid-run. Tears blurred my vision and as I regarded Morgana's fallen form, and without thinking I extended my hand in her direction and with all of my strength I pulled the branch out of her chest. As I continued to stand in the center of all the chaos, I witnessed the spirits of Morgana's ancestors, donning the ancient garb of the Druids embrace her spirit form as it rose from her fallen body. Our eyes met and for a millimeter of a second, she smiled before she disappeared.

"Maya look out!" Hacienda called out as she ran towards me. She waved her hands in front of me in a half circle and the protective shield went up just in time to block my mother's magic from snatching me.

"You dare get in between me and *my daughter*?" My mother hissed in Hacienda's direction.

"She is a child Marguerite," Hacienda snapped, taking position in front of me.

"Their house is divided!" One of Brixa's coven members shouted to the others. "Join hands. Combine our power. She will not leave here alive!"

"You bitches want power?" My mother chuckled darkly, her voice filtering into the deep spaces of our minds. "Allow me to introduce you to power in the flesh."

TWENTY-SIX

Silence fell upon the cemetery with the weight of a whisper. Our coven and the House of Brixa watched in terror as my mother smiled at the witches of the opposing coven, her eyes so dark one could see the flames of hell dancing about in her gaze. "At one point in time I would have defended any sister of magic against the devil himself," my mother seethed with clenched teeth. She kneeled down in the direction of the opposing coven. In my mind I saw the blackened and ever reaching tendrils that extended well beyond our blood line. Into the far reaches of the oblivion, she drew on the power of the ancient, dark magic, linked to us by Samael.

A shorter, yet older female stepped forward,

channeling her own power from the lightening that struck across the sky. Another came from behind her, both of her hands lit with a black flame. My heart pounded against my chest just as I pounded against the invisible prison that held me in place. I needed to do something. This had to stop. Another witch shouldn't have to die.

"Stop it!" I screamed. "Hacienda! Let me out! My magic will stop her! I can stop her!" My screams and cries fell on deaf ears. Even from behind Hacienda, I witnessed my mother funnel her dark energy into the ground. The soil, the grass, all of it turned black from her touch and spread out throughout the cemetery, indiscriminately creeping underneath the feet of all of us gathered. The first one to incinerate was the elder female, who acted a second too late with her power.

Hacienda turned around and removed the protective encasement from around me. She quickly hoisted me up and took off running at full speed.

Tell her to keep running! Annabelle whispered in my mind. *Help is here. Just keep moving.*

"Keep running Hacienda," I encouraged her.

"When I said I was going to get you out of here," Hacienda panted. "I meant it."

"Hacienda!" Janelle called out from behind. "They're here!"

"The other Guardians... yeah. I know. I just hope they know what they are up against."

"The others..." Janelle wheezed as we came to a stop at the entrance of the cemetery. "Bria, Camille... they are seriously wounded."

"I know. We lost Morgana and Beatrice too..."

"I never expected it to go this far."

"Me neither. What has gotten into her?"

"What's gotten into me is the fact that I have housed – for years mind you- a pair of treacherous, lecherous witches who have been actively conspiring against me with the very people," my mother's words boomed from behind the trees. "People who at one point in history would have burned the lot of us for less."

"Marguerite," Hacienda said, holding me tightly. "You will not use this child's power for your own gain. I don't care if she is your daughter."

"You low level witch you would dare challenge me? Marguerite Beauvais, the grand witch and High Priestess?!"

My mother's power trapped us in a circle of fire, the heat from the flames searing our flesh, singing our hair. Hacienda began to chant and with her spell she was able to dissipate the flames. Janelle fell to her knees and began to draw in the dirt with her finger, mapping a series of triangular and circular patters before yelling, "Maya! Go to the Crossroads like I taught you!"

But before I could even link my mind to Papa Legba's realm, a loud cracking sound interrupted my concentration. Hacienda's body went limp, her head twisted at an impossible angle. I fell from her arms, landing with a hard thud on my side. Pure horror filled me, paralyzing me next to Hacienda's lifeless body.

"Did you really think they were going to protect you, Maya?"

I couldn't move. I couldn't think. First Morgana, then Beatrice...now Hacienda and... Janelle released a soft squeak as she fell to her knees and her beating heart plopped to the ground.

"Did you really believe that I didn't know about your endless snooping? I knew you've been listening in on my private sessions with Samael. I know you have been communing with white light spirits to aid you. But let me tell you something, dear daughter, Samael, and I have an agreement – one that you will grow to understand must be honored."

The cry that I released from the center of my

chest perhaps echoed far into the bayous of Louisiana. My own mother could not stop me. She had gone too far. I gripped the sides of my head, overwhelmed by the noise that rattled the old mausoleums. I'm sure I even awakened the dead that day.

A pair of soft hands touched my shoulders from behind. In my mind's eye, I knew it was Annabelle. She gathered me in her arms and allowed me to rest my head on her chest.

I stopped screaming.

As my mother inched her way towards me, her expression ominous. I felt her reach for me, but the attempt was instantly thwarted by an iron dagger which pierced the hand that she reached for me with.

And then I heard them. The Guardians were closing in.

"I'm right here Maya," Annabelle cooed. "I told you I would never leave you...it's going to be ok."

TWENTY-SEVEN

Kinetic energy sent a wave of iron daggers in my mother's direction. Iron for a dark witch was what silver is to vampires. But instead of her turning to dust, it nullifies her magic, leaving her essentially about as defenseless as a normal human. My mother's mournful wail ricocheted throughout the cemetery as her blood dripped onto the grass along with her power. Her black blood left an acidic trail as she attempted to get away; but as more Guardians began to pour in, I knew that she could not escape the mess that she created.

"There is no way out of this one for you Marguerite," came a hooded figure who appeared from the shadows. "We have been watching you for a long time and you are just as bad as the vampires that we hunt.”

“Probably worse,” came a deeper voice from the side.

Annabelle kissed me on top of my head and disappeared, leaving me alone, still seated between Hacienda and Janelle’s fallen bodies. I leaned forward to touch Hacienda’s hand. Memories from our time spent together, her teaching me how to use earth magic, our trips to the park and random places whenever my mother allowed me the freedom to go... she was my friend.

And she died protecting me.

“I’m so sorry Hacienda...” I whimpered. “I’m so sorry Janelle for what she did to you.”

“That’s not your fault kid.”

I whipped my head around to meet the softened expression of someone I would learn to be the Primary Guardian, Archer Daniels. He looked down at me and slowly offered his hand.

“You must be Maya,” he said. “These are your friends?” He asked, nodding his head in Hacienda’s direction.

“Yes. They were my coven sisters and my... mother...”

“I know,” he continued. “It’s not your fault. You

are not to blame for what evil adults do – not even your parents."

"She wants to kill me too," I sobbed.

"I know all about that…your two friends here, came to us for help. They had a vision of what your mother was planning to do and to be honest, I'm glad they did." He smiled as I accepted his hand. "You are safe now."

My mother's shrieks boomed throughout the cemetery and into the street. Some of the other Guardians began to offer medical assistance to the survivors of my mother's rage. My mother began to chant, desperate to conjure a spell or some other magical assistance to free her from the iron cuffs that bound her.

"What is going to happen to her?" I meekly asked.

"She is going someplace where she won't have access to her power and where she can never hurt you or anyone again," Archer replied evenly.

"And where am I going to go?"

Archer sighed and kneeled down to my level. "Why don't we talk about that over some waffles? There is a special place for powerful kids like you to learn and grow. And judging by the environment you were living in, I take it there weren't many kids around, huh?"

I shook my head no, but my thoughts drifted back to Willow. Everything that happened this night, Willow's coven hoped to avoid. I learned later on after this night that nearly half of the opposing covens who appeared were killed. Some of them were not allowed proper burials due to the level of darkness my mother used against them. Their bodies were damned to infect whatever ground they were placed in. Instead, many of them were cremated and the remains had to be stored far away from potentially wicked hands to be used for even darker magic.

Archer helped me to my feet and calmly escorted me out of the burial grounds and safely secured me into the backseat of one of the black Sedans. A tall, muscular man with a bald head and warm smile approached us. I watched as he shook Archer's hand and the two exchanged quick pleasantries before he leaned in to get a closer view of me.

"Maya this is Congo," Archer said pointing at him. "He is one of us and probably one of the strongest mofos I know. He is also an expert on demons, but I am quite sure there is a lot you can teach him on the subject."

"Hi pretty girl," Congo began, extending his hand. "I'm going to sit here in the car with you while our buddy Archer finishes up over in the cemetery with the others."

"It won't be long," Archer promised me. "Oh, and Congo we are getting waffles after this with the little lady."

"Roger that. I'm starving. I heard New Orleans has some great places to eat at." He turned to look at me. "Know any good places?"

I paused before answering. I could only think of one place that would forever be branded as a childhood memory of mine.

"Pete's," I replied slowly.

Congo grinned and nodded his head. "Then Pete's it is."

TWENTY-EIGHT

Within twenty-four hours the House of Beauvais was no more. The Guardians came to what was once an immaculate multiroom estate with high vaulted ceilings, sitting room, game room, pantry space that a chef could envy, all of which that sat on land that dated back to the days of the indigenous peoples that once passed through its territory. Archer contacted my Uncle Kevin to request permission for a secret school and place of refuge for gifted humans known as The Vampire Hunters Academy to obtain custody of me. Uncle Kevin took the first flight out to meet us at the house of horror that was once my home to further discuss things. As it stood, no one knew who my biological father was, however as I reflect on these memories, I am pretty sure no one wanted to bother to look. And to be honest, I can't blame them. What would a human man do with a girl like me? A girl who could walk within the realms of life and death and come back unscathed? A girl who held dominion over demons…the same girl, who struggled with her own emotions which meant struggling to control my own power.

"She's too strong to be placed in a regular school that's for sure," Uncle Kevin admitted after an hour of rebuttals and refusals. "Definitely would hate to have to explain to her teacher how she turned one of her peers into a toad."

Archer chuckled as he continued to review the paperwork. "You will always be able to have contact with her. Once she is enrolled, she will be provided a personal cell phone, so she will always be able to contact you."

"Do you think that she has what it takes to become a Guardian?" Uncle Kevin asked curiously.

The question seemed to catch Archer off guard, he sputtered and stammered until he finally could put together the right words to best explain the overall purpose of the Academy. "She would have to work exceptionally hard. We do not typically accept witches of any kind, but every now and again, exceptions have to be made."

"In my line of work, I've come across quite a few Guardians," Uncle Kevin added. "I'm usually called upon to remove hexes and curses...I met one particular Guardian who made the mistake of sleeping with a real succubus and well... it took several cleansings to remove the root work she put on him."

"I know," Archer said reaching into his pocket for a pen. "I know all about you. You are our go to guy for healings and cleansings, given the line of work that we do, we need all the help we can get."

I continued to observe the two of them from across the room. Memories of my days spent in the different rooms of my coven sisters, learning about their magic and the techniques used to control their powers. It was in this front room where Morgana taught me about tarot. She even performed a reading on me once and one of the major cards that she pulled was the Magician. She told me that I was going to do great things one day and that I was lucky to be a part of such a powerful and diverse coven. To her I held an advantage that not many young witches did with my mother being one of them.

It saddened me to realize that she was sacrificed

for a cause she knew nothing about. The love that she had for all of us would now only serve as a memory. Uncle Kevin and Archer concluded their conversation with a friendly handshake. Uncle Kevin turned around and the sadness in his eyes made my heart hurt. He approached me slowly, stuffing his hands into the pockets of his favorite pair of faded jeans, stopping just in front of the coffee table that separated us.

"Looks like you got a new place to go kiddo," he said. "But at least you are now free."

"Where am I going? To that school Archer was talking about?" I asked, already knowing the answer. I just needed to hear him say it. I needed him to confirm that I would not be living with him and his family, that I would be going away where I would be out of sight and out of mind.

"Yes," he answered grimly. "But it is the best way to protect you. It is also the best place for you to learn your power so that one day, you might control it."

His gaze shifted to the ground the instant my heart sank. I darted off the couch and threw myself into his arms, wrapping myself around him as tightly as I could.

"I wanted to protect you," Uncle Kevin sobbed.

"I tried. I knew what she was going to do. Our grandmother was going to do the same thing to her, but she wasn't...accepted."

"She told me..." My mother's words returned to me, the horror of her truth regaining its hold on me. *"I was called to be the next Loa for our bloodline,"* she said softly.

"She was born with a dark soul," Uncle Kevin continued. "Even the Loa rejected her. Our mother – God rest her soul – did her best to try to protect us from the darkness that always seemed to follow. She even gave up her own magic with the hope that we could live normal lives... Unfortunately, magic is what ultimately killed her. Marguerite had grown far too powerful beyond even our mother's control."

My eyes widened at the realization at what happened to my grandmother. "I will never be like my mother. I will never hurt anyone!"

Uncle Kevin patted my head gently. "I know you won't," he told me. "You are nothing like Marguerite. You are kind and loving and hopeful... you have something that Marguerite in a million years will never have..."

"And what's that?" I sniffled, looking up at him.

He kneeled down to meet me at eye level. "Light.

You are a light for our bloodline Maya. That's what makes you so strong. Never forget that."

"I love you Uncle Kevin!"

"I love you too my little Maya. Train hard and learn as much as you can. You will do it for your old Uncle, right?"

I shook my head in agreement. "Yes. I'm going to make you proud."

"You already do Maya."

TWENTY-NINE

It took a few days before the day came for me to board my flight to Vatican City. Louisiana, New Orleans in particular, for all of its magic and horrors, mystery and mayhem, was a memory that I hoped to bury within the depths of my mind. I witnessed my own coven sisters die at the hands of my mother; the same mother who made a deal with a devil in exchange for power to sacrifice me on my sixteenth birthday. Louisiana was nothing more than a graveyard of nightmares. And as I surveyed every corner of my empty room, a spark of excitement for a new chapter made it easier for me to grab my new pink suitcase Uncle Kevin had bought me and turn towards the door.

"You are just not going to leave without saying

goodbye, are you?" Annabelle's form materialized in front of me. Her eyes red rimmed and filled with tears.

I released my suitcase and embraced her. "No. I thought you would always be with me… I thought you would join me at the Academy. I could never leave you without saying goodbye."

Annabelle wept. "I'm so happy for you Maya. Really, I am."

"What's wrong?" I asked, stepping away. "You are coming with me, right? You just can't let me go and be completely by myself…"

"You will never be alone again Maya," Annabelle cried. "But I can't go with you this time."

"What?" Now it was my turn for my eyes to fill with tears. "But you said-

"Remember what I told you? There is a girl that will be arriving at The Academy soon enough. She has a heavy weight on her shoulders just like you do."

"I can't do this without you! I don't want to go to The Academy without you Annabelle!"

Annabelle's gentle hand reached for my face and carefully collected a tear on her finger. "Your tears are diamonds from your soul, and you waste them. Save them."

"But…"

"Remember when I told you that I hoped to get my wings?" Annabelle asked softly, her gaze began to illuminate a delicate yellow light. A warm brighter light ignited within her and from her shoulders sprang a pair of massive white wings that stretched out, absorbing most of the empty space in the room. "I finally got my wings. Because of you, Maya, I got my wings." She smiled as more tears filled her eyes as I looked on in amazement. Annabelle had ascended, her purpose being fulfilled.

"Your wings are beautiful…" I gasped, reaching out to touch a single feather. My glance returned to her face; her ethereal beauty transcended anything anyone could imagine. "You are going to be the best angel that Heaven will ever know!" I declared, cheerfully.

Annabelle laughed, her giggle sounding more like the wind chimes that used to hang in Hacienda's window. "And your name will be written in the stars in the book of Legends. I will continue to check in on you when I can. But you are free to be whoever you want to be." She hugged me tightly, enveloping me in her wings. "I love you always. But now, it is time for you to walk into your purpose Maya. You are free."

It was odd to be surrounded by complete strangers but still feel so loved and protected at the same time. Uncle Kevin accompanied me to the airport, riding in the Sedan with me and the other Guardians. He was quiet for most of the ride, lost in his thoughts just as I was lost in my mine. When we arrived at the airport, he bought me donuts and sat with me until it was time to board.

Archer came forward and offered Kevin a handshake. "She will call you as soon as we land," he promised. "I will email you the itinerary of her school schedule and see to it that you are kept up to date on her progress."

"Thank you," Uncle Kevin muttered. "Thank you so much."

"We also let the neighboring team of Guardians in your area know to keep an eye out on you and your family," Archer continued as he reached into his pocket and handed my uncle a brand new cell phone. "This has all of my contact information, including those that you met with already and the Guardians that will be protecting you and your family. You and Maya are one of us now and we always protect our own."

My uncle nodded as he accepted the phone. "I will be waiting for her call."

Uncle Kevin leaned down and kissed me on my forehead. "I love you, Maya. Try not to give the other students too much hell – well, maybe just a little if they deserve it."

Both Archer and my uncle shared a laughed as I hugged him for what would feel like the final time.

"Now boarding flight 51C, American Airlines…" The announcer blasted from the speakers.

"It's time," Archer announced as he extended his hand, which I accepted. "You ready Maya?"

I tearfully nodded my head as my uncle gave me two thumbs up.

"Ok. Let's go."

I waved goodbye to my uncle, who was the last remaining of my bloodline, and the last of those, at least in Louisiana, that loved me. I found comfort in Archer's hand and strangely enough, I didn't want to let it go – at least, not until we reached our destination.

And he didn't let go. He held my hand the entire sixteen hours, even when I fell asleep on his shoulder. Annabelle was right. Everything was going to be ok.

EPILOGUE

Eleven years later...

September 30, 2015

"Ay who is the new girl?" Rider, one of the advanced Guardian trainees asked me as we took our seats in the cafeteria. Why he decided to sit at the same table as me, along with his bandit of idiot bastards was beyond me.

I looked up at the girl who nervously stood at the end of the tray line. Her long braids hung freely to her waist; her rich brown skin held its own special glow to it. For a moment, I envied her beauty. She would definitely stand out here in the Academy and what was worse she would instantly be a target for Elizabeth Van Helzing's never ending harassment and beratement. But still, she carried a power unique to her and none that I had detected in any of the Guardians. Who was she?

"First of all, why are you even this close to me?" I spat, no longer interested in the spaghetti that was served for lunch.

"The hell is wrong with you Myra? Damn, it's a free world," Rider fired back.

"Chill out," Myra, one of the senior Guardians scolded. "We have a new student. Please act like you have some home training."

"Who is she?" I asked curiously, continuing to watch her as she collected a small plate and utensils.

"She is what this school has been waiting for," Myra said proudly. "We found her two days ago. Her father came home as a vampire and killed her mother. He might have killed her too had Tatsu not arrived in time." Myra paused and looked over at me. "I think you two will get along perfectly."

"She would be better off hanging with us," Rider scoffed. "Maya doesn't like people too much – that's why she doesn't have any friends."

"You can go straight to hell Rider or better yet, how about I help send you there?"

"Maya!" Myra scolded. "Are you hoping to find yourself back in detention?"

"Well, he always fu- starts with me," I protested.

"That doesn't mean you always have to respond. You are better than that." Myra gave Rider a hard glare. "Why don't you and your cronies find another table for now. I need to talk to Maya."

Rider groaned but said nothing more as he and his friends packed up their trays and headed towards the empty tables on the far end of the room.

"She's just like you when you first came here: angry, heartbroken, and scared, her powers began manifesting too early and what was worse her parents had no idea of what she was becoming. They didn't even know vampires existed – until they were faced with the misfortune of finding out the hard way."

"What if she doesn't like me? Nobody else does," I shrugged. I hated the school. I couldn't wait for the day that I could strike out on my own. It didn't matter what anybody said, there was no way I would ever become a Guardian. Most of the Guardians kept their distance from me anyways.

"Oh, trust me. You and her will be best friends in no time," Myra said with a reassuring grin. She waved at the new girl and motioned for her to join us at our table. "If you stop pushing people away, Maya, you won't feel so isolated. It isn't your magic that people are afraid of. We know what you are, and we love you anyways. Now…"

As the girl approached our table, I could feel Elizabeth's dagger-like stare sizing her up and down. But I knew as soon as our gaze met, that there was something in her spirit that I could trust. Maybe, Myra was right. She smiled weakly at Myra who quickly performed our introductions.

"Maya this Sanaya, Sanaya this is Maya."

"Hi, Maya," Sanaya said offering her hand. "Archer told me about you," she started to chuckle.

"And what did he say?" I said quickly, looking at her hand.

"He said you pretty much keep this campus lit and not a day goes by that he doesn't frown or shake his head… He said you will be the cause of his death or early retirement." She burst out with laughter, laughter that was too infectious to not join in.

"What can I say?" I shrugged. "I like to keep things interesting."

And just like that we were joined at the hip, so much so that I abandoned my own private quarters to bunk in hers. On one particular day, I sat on a bench in the courtyard, our usual meet up spot, while waiting for Sanaya to finish up with her English class. As I waited, I felt the familiar, gentle whisper of a spirit that I would never forget. Annabelle.

I told you that you would never be alone again Maya. But now I am here to tell you that now that you and our Huntress have finally linked paths, the journey that your dark path has prepared you for, has now begun. Train hard. Fight hard. And just as I promised you many, many times, I will be with you...always.

OTHER BOOKS BY DELIZHIA JENKINS

THE VAMPIRE HUNTERS ACADEMY SERIES

The Darkness

The Shadows

The Reckoning

The Cursed

The Forsaken

Cain

STANDALONES:

Sanctum: A Last Huntress Novel

Rise of the Elites House of the Blue Flame

The Lost Queen Mercury's Heir

Out of the Shadows

Into the Shadows

Raphael

In the Light of Darkness

Blind Salvation

Viper The Vampire Assassin

Sin Daughter of the Grim Reaper

Love At Last

Nubia Rising: The Awakening

ANTHOLOGIES:

Dark Moon Curse, Black Magic Woman

Frostbite, Slay

Ready to Join the Vampire Hunters Academy? For exclusive content and sneak peeks into The Vampire Hunters Academy, become a Patreon member by signing up today:

The Vampire Hunters Academy is creating Blogs, diaries and journals and books | Patreon

For more about the author, visit missjenkinsbooks.com

ABOUT THE AUTHOR

Delizhia Jenkins is an Urban Fantasy and Paranormal Romance author who currently resides in Inglewood, CA. The love for writing began in elementary school when the passion for storytelling developed into a journey of writing. Over the years, she honed her craft for storytelling and the written word by excelling in subjects such English and English Literature; and by indulging in her favorite past time which involved reading the works of Anne Rice, K'Wan, Christopher Pike, Carl Weber, Omar Tyree and finally the late L.A. Banks. J.R. Ward's *Black Dagger Brotherhood* also claimed her heart and author Karen Marie Moning joined the ranks of Miss Jenkins' all-time favorite authors.

Miss Jenkins began publishing in 2013 with her first African American romance novel, *Love at Last.* After that, it was realized that her true magic rested in her writing about the ancient, the esoteric, and the supernatural. Moreover, since 2014, after her release of Nubia Rising: The Awakening, Miss

Jenkins remained true to herself and her calling. And of course, being a true romantic at heart, it was important for her to fuse romance with the paranormal with a dash of "color." Miss Jenkins prides herself on writing for "the woman without the fairytale" and of course bringing magic and melanin to each book she writes.

Follow Miss Jenkins on the following platforms

Twitter: @septembershope or hunters_vampire
Join my email list: missjenkinsbooks.com

facebook.com/DJenkinsbooks
twitter.com/hunters_vampire
instagram.com/miss_jenkins_books
tiktok.com/@authordelizhia